# Fireflies and Cosmos

Interstellar Spring Book 1

by J. Darris Mitchell

Other Books by J. Darris Mitchell

Interstellar Spring

Diamondcrabs and Mangoes

Iceoaks and Warblers

Pricklypears and Tarantula Hawks*

The Wild Lands

The Legend of the Wild Man

*forthcoming

This book represents hours and hours of work done by the author as well as many other people he both loves and respects. Don't steal it. If you are interested in sharing it contact the author and he will be happy to assist you. It violates the sacred bond of writer and reader to reproduce or reprint any part of this book without the author's written permission, except for brief quotations in critical reviews. In other words, reprinting or reproducing this book is illegal. It's totally OK to let a friend read this copy, but please direct them to the website so they can purchase the rest of the series themselves and thus help the author and those in his life put food on their tables.

Thank you.

This is a work of fiction. All of the characters, events and organizations are either imagined by the author or used fictiously.

INTERSTELLAR SPRING: *FIREFLIES AND COSMOS*

Copyright 2017 by J. Darris Mitchell

All rights reserved

Cover Art by Sam Mayle
Find more at https://sammaylearts.myportfolio.com/

Independently Published
ISBN 9781521008058

www.jdarrismitchell.com

*For Raquel*

*Without whom
there would be no flowers
on the 51 Seeded Worlds*

# CONTENTS

Fireflies and Cosmos ............................................................. 1
1. ........................................................................................ 7
2. ...................................................................................... 12
3. ...................................................................................... 15
4. ...................................................................................... 18
5. ...................................................................................... 22
6. ...................................................................................... 29
7. ...................................................................................... 36
8. ...................................................................................... 39
9. ...................................................................................... 44
10. .................................................................................... 47
11. .................................................................................... 52
12. .................................................................................... 57
13. .................................................................................... 64
14. .................................................................................... 69
15. .................................................................................... 75
16. .................................................................................... 82
17. .................................................................................... 89

| | |
|---|---|
| 18. | 94 |
| 19. | 101 |
| 20. | 105 |
| 21. | 110 |
| 22. | 114 |
| 23. | 117 |
| Acknowledgements | 124 |
| Diamondcrabs and Mangoes | 125 |

# 1

One might think *Homo sapiens* would have shrugged off an ailment as old and simple as heartbreak long ago, but this was simply not the case.

Captain Catalina Solaris Xao Mondragon looked down upon the swirling clouds of Bulletar from the deck of the *Artemis* with apprehension. Through the cloud cover of the tropical planet she saw forests grown from seeds planted here by autonomous machines decades ago and between them, huge plazzglass domes—great half-spheres that contained cities dense with people. When she'd left Roman Luz Jupiter down there she'd told him that he would never set foot on her ship again. It was a small consolation that the ship she now captained was a different ship.

'Permission to speak freely, sir?'

Captain Mondragon turned to her first officer, Farah Relkor, and raised an eyebrow. 'What happens if I say no?' Though Farah's tall and thin frame towered over the short and curvaceous captain, Catalina Mondragon was not in the least bit intimidated by her old friend.

'You'll be forced to mark me for insubordination in your record, sir,' Farah said, her thin lips struggling to hold back a vicious grin.

'You'd risk another mark on your record?'

'Sir, with all due respect, if we are here for the reason I believe us to be, my comments will prove to be far from the most egregious violation committed aboard this ship.'

Captain Mondragon looked at Farah Relkor standing at attention aboard the tiny bridge. Though her crew was small by most standards, she knew they were the best in the inhabited sector. Farah Relkor and her husband, Kensei 'Ikamon' Mizuyama, were the most passionate Interstellar Ecologists she'd ever met, and it didn't hurt that even after so many years of marriage they were able to work through any stressful situations in the most carnal, if not quietest, of methods.

Her pilot, Fin, was fresh from Earth-3, but Captain Mondragon had already seen enough of her maneuvers on Epsilon-V to know she was a valuable asset. It was a pity they'd lost Dr. Mercurian on Epsilon-V; that was what had brought them here. Fin's fast actions had saved their lives and the ship, but she hadn't been able to save the doctor. No one could have, not in the face of those...those aberrations. Catalina only hoped that she wasn't making a mistake. She respected her crew of three and valued their opinions and skills, but there were times when she wished Farah was a bit more tactful. Captain Mondragon sighed.

'Say what you must.'

'When it comes to Roman Jupiter,' Farah said, 'I'd prefer to have it on the record that I find him an unprofessional, easily distracted, incompetent, womanizing moron. He made your last ship less efficient by a magnitude of ten, and I think leaving him on Bulletar was one of the smartest things you ever did, both professionally and personally.'

Captain Mondragon could tell from the tone of her first officer's voice that Farah was only getting started. Her pale eyes were burning, and her thin lips twitched at the sides, desperately trying to hide her snarky grin.

'Wait, what do you mean *personally*? I've never seen the captain be anything but professional,' Fin said. She punched something into the command console at the head of the bridge and turned to face the two women. Her short, pink hair was still black at the tips from her last dye-job and her bangs covered one eye. Her button of a nose pointed up, right at Catalina.

Captain Mondragon bristled—she knew she should have said something sooner, that this conversation was inevitable, that Farah had a right to know, that her crew had a right to know, but this way, she had hoped to at least minimize the time she would have to hear Farah bitch about the decision. But she had no choice. Despite everything else Roman was, he was a damn gifted Entomologist, and a survey ship—even one as special as the *Artemis*—could not perform its duties unless it could successfully sample bacteria, plants, fungi, fish, mollusks, and bugs. Kensei was a master of the seas, and Farah a keen Botanist, but neither knew a sphinx moth from a swallowtail. It had to be this way, especially after the horror they had seen on Epsilon-V.

'What is happening? I heard yelling,' Kensei said softly as he stepped onto the bridge and joined the rest of the crew. Kensei was the living antithesis to his wife. He had pale skin and dark eyes, nearly as black as his hair, while Farah's skin was caramel colored, her eyes pale, and her hair the color of sun-bleached straw. Both were thin, and had the ropy muscles of regular, repetitive exercises, but their similarities ended there. While Farah always had to make an effort to conceal her simmering emotions, Kensei was relaxed and easygoing. Even in their work ethic they differed; Farah labored in dirty coveralls while Kensei preferred to swim through his aquariums in nothing but a speedo. When he wore his uniform, it was always as spotless as the captain's. That two people so different could stay together after traveling so much of the inhabited sector was a testament to the power of love. Kensei seemed to have a natural ability to tell when Farah was about to explode, and could, almost without fail, diffuse her. Captain Mondragon had only seen Kensei fail in his ability to calm Farah once before, but it seemed that, at this moment, that gift was going to go unused. Kensei looked from his wife to Fin, who was smiling devilishly at the captain. He cocked his head.

'Captain,' he said in slightly accented English, 'is there a problem?'

'First Officer Relkor is going on the record about her issues with picking up a man from Bulletar because of the personal relationship between him and the captain. At least, that's what I've got so far.' Fin's eyes gleamed with the gossip.

Kensei chuckled. 'So...Bulletar is where we are to get our Entomologist, or should I say, our ex-Entomologist?'

'Wait, what?' Fin said.

At that moment, despite all Catalina had seen her crew do, despite all the worlds they had visited together in the last year, despite the ecosystems they had saved where ships crewed with dozens had failed, despite their history of successfully upholding the Charter, Catalina hated all of them.

'Oh come on! Who is this guy?' Fin said.

'Roman Jupiter is a talented, albeit unorthodox Entomologist,' Captain Mondragon said. 'He is a passionate, hardworking man who is uniquely qualified to assist us on our mission of surveying the 51 Seeded Worlds that the Institute began terraforming nearly a century ago. Given our situation, and the loss of Dr. Mercurian, I see no alternative.'

'Oh cut the crap, Cat. Fin has a right to know. Roman Jupiter is a beer-guzzling, hormonal idiot driven by only two things in life: fornicating with a woman from every inhabited planet, and catching fireflies. He is hairy, smelly, easily distracted, and he broke the captain's heart.'

# 2

'The captain had a boyfriend? I've never seen her so much as look at a man!' Fin blurted.

Despite her light brown skin, Captain Catalina Solaris Xao Mondragon turned a bright shade of crimson.

'Oh, that's because she hasn't since she was with Roman,' Farah replied. 'How did it end, Catalina? Oh that's right, exactly the same way it did every other time he ended a relationship. We went to a new planet, he saw some tawny, buxom bimbo, and forgot all about the last girl whose heart he ripped in half.'

'Roman cannot help himself, and you cannot deny he possesses much entomological skill,' Kensei said.

'He gets the job done, I'll give him that,' Farah said. 'But his head is filled with untestable questions and half-baked promises. And if I *ever* hear you refer to women the same way you'd refer to free samples at an open-air market, I swear it to the *Artemis* we won't bang for a month. Captain, he will do what he always does, he will try to seduce you until we find another planet, where he'll forget all about you until we leave, his loins sated, his collection of fireflies having added another damn bug.'

'First Officer Relkor, your objections are noted. That is quite enough,' Captain Mondragon said.

'I don't know how you expect us to work with him. What if he tries to seduce Fin?' Farah's voice possessed more than a tinge of rage.

'Trust me, you don't have to worry about that,' Fin mumbled.

'I can't believe you dragged us all the way across the sector for this!' Farah was losing control.

'There is no other choice,' Captain Mondragon said, her words so cold they could be shattered. 'We cannot hope to fulfill the Charter unless we have the very best crew possible. Roman is the only Entomologist I know of whose skills are equal to the other members of this crew. You remember what we saw on Epsilon-V. Those things tore Patrick apart. For all we know, every outer world could be filled with creatures far more dangerous than those bugs.'

'Well at least there's solace in that. Maybe if we go back to Epsilon-V those bugs can finish with Roman what they started with the late Doctor,' Farah said.

Before the words had even echoed off the walls of the *Artemis*, Captain Mondragon saluted her old friend and said, 'First Officer and Ship Botanist Farah Relkor, you are dismissed of all duties for the next six hours.'

'Cat...I didn't mean that. I didn't know you still had feelings for Roman.'

'First Officer, you are dismissed. Must I order our second officer to escort you to your quarters?'

Farah looked from Catalina to Kensei, who only shrugged and shook his head.

'Captain, I'm sorry,' Farah managed, before she turned and marched off the bridge.

For a moment there was only silence, then something beeped from the console of the *Artemis* and Fin turned back to her duties.

'Captain, they have approved our landing request. You want me to go ahead?'

'Affirmative, Fin. Proceed to landing center Delta, notify me when we land. I will be in my quarters.'

'Yes, sir.'

'Captain,' Kensei ventured, 'if I may—'

'I understand your wife's concerns and respect her wishes to make them known. In truth, it is I that should apologize, I should have told you all sooner. I'm sorry, Officer Mizuyama.'

'No, Captain, it is not that. She was not in line, and please, you know I hate that name.'

Catalina nodded. 'Do you wish to note a concern as well?'

Ikamon shrugged, then seemed to remember himself and saluted, 'No, Captain. I have never doubted your judgment, neither professionally nor personally. Neither does Farah. It is just that she gets worked up about such things.'

'I know, Kensei. It's fine. If there's nothing else, I'll be in my quarters.'

Kensei nodded and Catalina turned to go.

'Uh, Captain, it's just that—'

'Yes, Officer Ikamon?' Captain Mondragon whirled and Kensei shrank back from her gaze

'I never thought he smelled that bad, and he *was* always correct about the fireflies. Even on Epsilon-V, you know? I think perhaps our history together is what makes us such a strong team. Perhaps your past with Jupiter will prove to be advantageous as well.'

'Thank you, Kensei,' Catalina said, and retired to her chamber before Fin lost control and started to ask far too many questions.

# 3

Catalina dearly hoped that she was not making a mistake as she straightened the badges of distinction on her uniform, then knocked on Farah's door.

The door yanked open and Catalina immediately realized her hopes would not be coming true.

Farah Relkor stood there in what on some planets would be called lingerie, and on others would surely be illegal. She had on thigh-high leather heels, a black thong, and a black leather bra studded with silver spikes that cupped her small breasts exceptionally well. In her hand she held a switch, and her eyes glowed with malevolent intent. That was, until she saw the captain standing in her doorway.

'Captain!' she saluted, dropping the whip, then picking it back up and attempting to use it to cover the parts of her that weren't hidden by leather straps. 'I...you said I was dismissed.'

'I wanted to apologize, but clearly this is not a good time,' Catalina said.

'No, it's fine! I was just expecting Ken.'

'I put him on docking duty. I wanted to talk to you, but I will send him right in.'

'No! No, Captain, that won't be necessary. His duty is to our mission first and me second. It's just, if I could slip into something, uh...less comfortable?'

Catalina nodded and a few minutes later found herself sipping a warm mug of tea with a much more thoroughly covered Farah Relkor. Her mind still wandered to Farah's neckline and wondered at her body beneath, now hidden in a thick and unbecoming silk kimono. Catalina found herself wondering if Farah had changed out of her leather bondage gear and now sat with her on the couch naked beneath the robe, or if she still wore the elaborate leather lingerie. Catalina sighed inwardly, thinking of the last time she had dressed to tantalize a man. It had been for Roman.

'Captain, I would like to apologize for my appearance,' Farah said, her voice a little too loud.

'Farah, don't be silly, and you can call me Cat. I dismissed you, remember? You're not on duty, and I'm in *your* chambers clearly interrupting *your* evening. I feel I owe you an apology, I should have told you sooner about our mission, about Roman.'

Farah rolled her eyes at the mention of his name, but kept her composure. 'No. I should apologize. You're right, Roman is a good Entomologist, and if we're going back out there, we'll need the very best. And besides, Ken may be skilled with a knife, but I could go for some protein besides fish. Roman always could make a mean bug burger.'

Catalina smiled. 'You know I wouldn't crew him if I didn't feel it absolutely necessary.'

Farah nodded. 'Yes, Captain, I understand. The Institute needs us to survey and prove that the 51 Seeded Worlds have air, water, and healthy soil or sea before the centennial, and before the Big Three Corporations try to stake a claim. I get it. If we don't survey them in a "prompt and timely manner" the Corps will, and we both know all they give a shit about is how quickly and how many domes and prefabs they can cram on a planet. I mean, can you imagine if one of their D-classes showed up on Epsilon-V with those damn digital probes? There's no way they would've found those bugs burrowed under the surface. If the Doctor hadn't noticed their trails, and the Corps had started to build, who knows what could have happened?'

'That's exactly why I need Roman,' Catalina said. 'He's good. He's always been good. I know we have a history, but I will not let that stand between this ship and its mission. The *Artemis* is uniquely suited to this task, and I believe Roman will be a real asset.'

'Yeah, and you'd be a real idiot to let him break your heart twice, right?'

Catalina gritted her teeth and reminded herself Farah was off duty.

'I thought that what we had was different—that since we could travel together between the stars he wouldn't fall in love with a new woman every month. I thought we could be like you and Ken.'

Farah laughed. 'Roman is about as far from Ken as possible. He is hairy, dirty, easily distracted, un-methodical, and he stinks. Shit, they even prepare food differently. Ken never cooks a damn thing, and Roman fries all his little buggies to a crisp. It won't be so bad. Just promise me you won't fall for him again.'

Catalina raised an eyebrow.

'Captain, I would like to submit a formal apology for my actions. I was out of line to doubt you,' Farah said as she stood and saluted crisply. Catalina noticed that the leather high heels, at least, she had not removed.

'Your formal apology is noted and rejected. You were right. I should have told you, I just wish you hadn't brought it up in front of Fin.'

Farah smiled. 'Can you imagine? What if he falls for her?'

'Then we jettison him into deep space.'

# 4

The *Artemis* was a ship designed with a purpose. Between control panels and consoles, every centimeter of every wall was made of plazzglass enclosures filled with plants, fish, mollusks, or insects collected from the Seeded Worlds. A century ago, the Institute's mission had been simply to see which of the organisms loaded onto the Seedpods and shot into space had survived and which combinations of plants and animals made for the most habitable ecosystems for people, but after a time Interstellar Ecologists like Catalina's father had quickly seen there was more to surveying work than simply cataloging what they already knew. That might work for the Corps' survey ships, but the *Artemis* had the capability to do far more than store digital records.

On every planet they went to, they discovered creatures that had, under the light of a different sun and with a different atmospheric mix to breathe, evolved and conquered worlds. Each of the 51 Seedpods had been loaded with the same couple thousand different organisms and identical team of robotic gardening machines, and yet—in a scant hundred years—each planet had evolved its own unique ecology. Some planets had oceans that teamed with brightly colored fish unlike any seen on Earth-1, others had strange mollusks with shells and tentacles beyond what mankind had ever imagined. There were always familiar species of insects, bees, ants and the like, but they often behaved in strange ways or had specialized to some quirk of the planet's geography. Nearly every planet had strangely shaped and oddly colored versions of the plants back home.

The *Artemis* was to build a library of the entire galaxy.

After a decade of exploration, Captain Mondragon had returned to Earth-1 to be promoted to captain and been placed in charge of this cutting-edge vessel owned by the Institute for Organic Expansion. The first member of her crew was already on board. Fin's flight instructors gave her sterling praise, and when Catalina found out that Fin had applied to work on the *Artemis* and no other ship, she had agreed to take the young pilot on the first test flight of her new vessel. Fin proved she could control the ship with ability that was almost supernatural. When she was also able to explain how the various automated engineering systems worked—its oxygen processors comprised entirely of species of plants and algae instead of the standard carbon-sink converters on most vessels, the odd orientation of its artificial gravity, its bizarre bacterial engines that could use sunlight to make fuel that could warp space and make faster-than-light travel possible—Catalina had canceled her other interviews. She could hardly wrap her head around what she'd been given. It seemed that there were too many high-hoped, outlandish ideas on one vessel for it to possibly work.

When Catalina had first been assigned to the ship and given permission to crew it with whomever she wished, she'd wondered if the Institute had hoped that the whole thing would run out of sugar in between stars and simply float off into nothingness never to be seen again, but her crew disproved that nightmare time and time again. Farah Relkor, Kensei Ikamon Mizuyama, the talented Fin, and the late Dr. Patrick Mercurian had saved countless lives, and helped the Institute hold up its end of the Charter on close to a dozen worlds. They had been to every inner planet: the star systems closest to Earth and most accessible by Bubbledrive. They had learned to use the awesome capabilities of the *Artemis* to clone bacteria, modify insects, and spawn fish so that the Institute's hundred-year-old promise of fresh air, clean water, and either healthy sea or soil, had been upheld. No one had told the captain to do this at first; her mission had been one of collector, but when her superiors had seen what the young Mondragon could do with this living library, they had released her to answer distress calls and pick her own missions.

Catalina only hoped her current detour wouldn't prove to be a waste of time.

Humanity had flourished in the Interstellar Spring, as it was called, and was now poised for what the Institute called the "Second Spring." Five worlds held Earth's name, thriving colonies of close to a billion each. Another dozen worlds were inhabited by millions of people edging ever closer to the manufacturing capabilities present on Earths 1-5, and dozens more remained on the fringes of inhabited space waiting to be colonized.

Every one of these outer planets needed to be surveyed to find out if the Seedpods had been successful, to see what life had made of the planet, or if life had made it at all. Dead worlds had been discovered, even among the inner planets, and as they moved farther and farther from Earth-1 what they would see would be ever less predictable, or at least, that was the case if Epsilon-V was any indication. If Catalina was going to continue to do that work, continue to find new life forms and uphold the Charter to protect life in all its forms, both human and otherwise, from the relentless grind of the Corps and their burbdomes, she would need an Entomologist. And there was no man better with bugs than Roman.

Captain Mondragon sighed deeply and leaned against the wall of her ship, hardly flinching when she touched moss. It simply meant Farah Relkor's experiments were going well.

'Captain, are you sure about this?' Farah asked.

'We don't have any other choice. Kensei, you said you kept in touch?'

'Yes, Captain...I have, eh...heard tell of his...exploits,' Kensei said. 'I would have notified him in advance if you had told me.'

'If I didn't tell the two of you we were coming here, I certainly wouldn't tell him.'

'Yes, Captain,' Kensei replied, making no attempt to hide his smile.

'Pilot Fin, you got the ship?'

'Aye-aye, Captain.'

'Well then by all means, Mr. Ikamon, lead the way.'

# 5

They followed the map on Ikamon's tablet down straight streets that ran between towering, rectangular skyscrapers. High up above the synthetic force field that served as a sky and glowed a harsh, artificial blue. Catalina found herself wondering what could have possibly compelled Roman Jupiter of all people to live in a corporate burbdome. The cities had no natural bodies of water, no plants, and no insects. Catalina thought of them as huge factories where people moved to pretend like they were living somewhere more rugged than Earth-1, but in reality the Domes were far more sterile than Earth-1 had ever been. Housing people was the singular purpose of the burbdomes, and in Catalina's opinion, even that they did poorly. There were no natural places, no plants, not even manicured lawns or carefully trimmed trees. The wealthy chose to live either in the towering heights of the buildings tall enough to actually graze the artificial ceiling, or near the edge of the dome's shield, far from what realtors marketed as the energizing "hustle and bustle" of automated cars, trains, and gravbuses. The corporations claimed the burbdomes were far safer than living off the land and under the Charter, and the data was beginning to support them. They'd only had one cataclysmic failure—a total system collapse on Texas that had cost millions of lives—but that was over a decade ago and the Corps had fixed the anomaly, or so they claimed. Still, Catalina didn't trust the things. Burbdomes felt claustrophobic to her, despite the towering buildings and far-away force field. They felt as if life went there to die.

That was one of the reasons she loved her job so much: because she was upholding the Charter, and ensuring that people had a right to live off the soil and the sea with their own two hands instead of clustered together in one of these prefabs. That was also one of the reasons she respected her crew so much—they were Naturalists who detested sanitized dome life almost as much as they loved getting their hands dirty studying the wild ecology of the 51 Seeded Worlds. That passion was also one of the reasons she had fallen in love with Roman, and what made his residency here that much more troubling to her.

The crew of the *Artemis* trekked past countless buildings distinguishable only by the ever-increasing digits until they arrived at 143,571. Far more people than that lived on Bulletar. It was one of the inner planets, after all, and had been established decades before the Corps had perfected their burbdome cities. Plenty of people still lived outside, fishing and farming for their sustenance, mining ore, trying to make something of themselves instead of just a data cruncher or pencil pusher for the big Corps. Catalina sighed. She had imagined a hunt through the wilderness to retrieve Roman from somewhere out in the wild. Instead, he was in a box with a number on a door that was left slightly ajar.

Kensei, seeing this breach of etiquette, went to knock, but Farah quickly caught his hand.

'I heard voices,' she said, and leaned in.

Despite her professionalism, Catalina found herself putting her ear to the empty door.

'Your legs and arms are florescent petals and I am but a viceroy butterfly, transfixed by this beauty. Never before have

I seen skin like yours. Never again will I lay eyes on a beauty so sweet. We are meant for each other, pollen and pollinator, each wondering which initiated this fantastic romance, and each knowing it will never end—'

'Yeah, about that,' said a higher-pitched female voice.

'Time knows no limits save eternity, and not until I met you did I understand what "endless" could truly mean.'

'Roman, we need to talk,' the woman said flatly.

'Then talk, my dear, and like the drops of rain echoing in the forests as they splash off of the petals of a delicate jungle flower, I will hear every sound and it will all wash over me.'

'Roman, I don't think we should be together anymore.'

'Mm...Captain,' Kensei said and cleared his throat, 'perhaps we should knock.'

'Shut up, Ken, this is gonna be good!' Farah said, and elbowed him in the ribs.

'—but a bee cannot survive without its flower,' Roman finished.

'That's the thing. You're always going on about bees, lightning bugs, spiders, but you live in this city with me. Maybe you belong out there,' the woman said patiently.

'But, my love, we've been over this. You detest the natural world. It's one of the reasons why you moved here, away from our nest of hammocks near the equator.'

'Yes, you're right. I don't like the natural world, but you do. We don't have a lot in common. I mean, don't you miss the flowers?' Even from outside, Captain Mondragon could tell the woman was annoyed, yet Roman blithely answered, seemingly oblivious to her disinterest.

'Of course, I do, that is why I have brought a flower to you! Behold, our apartment can be filled with the sweet aromas of the jungle, like the extinct Monarchs of Earth-1, I can migrate back and forth between the jungle and our home, bringing you gifts ever sweeter, until it feels that we are again in the wild.'

'That's not legal, Roman. The cities are supposed to be clean.' Her tone of voice made it sound as if they'd been over this many times before.

'This flower will but clean the air and leave a delicate aroma that is far sweeter than those Ortho-scents you insist on buying.'

'You *did* get rid of those!'

'They are artificial and entirely unappealing flavors, my buttercup. This lily, harvested deep in the rain-canyons of the south, is far sweeter and more subtle than those manufactured odors.'

'I don't want subtle, I want the Ortho-scent I bought! You stink, Roman! And your flower doesn't smell any better.'

'Told you he stinks,' Farah hissed. Before Catalina could reply, however, they heard what was probably the aforementioned flowerpot smash to pieces.

'And I'm sick of your hair clogging the drain and your poetry about nature. I'm sick of it all! I just want a break!'

Perhaps it wasn't the flowerpot, for something else crashed against the wall.

'But, my darling, how can a poor viceroy hope to survive if—'

Something far heavier smashed against the ground. Catalina actually felt the apartment shake.

'I don't care about the viceroys or gypsy moths, and I give zero shits about you or your damn fireflies!'

With that, the door flung open and the woman strode out and stood between Catalina, Farah, and Kensei without seeming to notice them. She was close to two meters tall, had short, bleached hair, a nose ring, and tremendously large breasts. In her hand, she held a jar with a single stick and a lonely firefly that blinked its abdomen weakly in the harsh glare of the artificial light. She raised the jar up above her head and hurled it to the ground. It shattered between the feet of the crew of the *Artemis*. The woman went back inside and, from the sound of it, began to trash the rest of their home.

Roman, it seemed, had finally heard enough. He dashed out of the apartment and fell to his knees between the trio of voyeurs. Catalina cleared her throat to speak, but Roman didn't notice her any more than the hulking woman had. Instead he very gently, almost daintily, snatched the firefly out of the air and cautiously tucked it into a small vial that he pulled out of his pocket. The insect being safe, he immediately turned back to the door, which had been slammed shut in the brief moment he'd left the apartment, and began to pound upon it.

'Darling Betriz, please let me in! I know you're mad! But think of the poor honeybee left without a hive, lonely it wanders until it, too, succumbs to that most devastating of all ailments—heartbreak!'

Betriz had apparently heard enough of this, and now only wanted to listen to the sounds of whatever possessions Roman had once owned smash to bits.

Catalina, seemingly shaken from her stupor, put a hand on Roman's shoulder.

'Jupiter!'

He turned to face her, and it was as if she was meeting him for the first time all over again. He was tall and broad shouldered, with unruly, dark brown hair that managed to make his neat haircut look messy. His strong nose was a mountain between the two oceans that were his gorgeous, brown eyes. He was clean shaven, but already a healthy shade of stubble graced his cheeks. He looked at Catalina and for a moment said nothing, then grinned his big, wicked grin. With that smile, Catalina didn't feel as if she was seeing him for the first time. She remembered everything that smile meant to Roman—skinny dipping in alien waterfalls, chasing fireflies into moonlit fields, and the glow of it aboard their last ship, the

*R.L. Carson,* when they'd both been but crew, and against her better judgment Catalina had slept with a junior officer.

'Sola, I haven't seen you since the trek between Tenagra and Bulletar.'

Catalina Solaris Xao Mondragon remembered much of their time together, but she had forgotten that he'd always called her Sola. She might have lost it at that moment, thrown her arms around him despite all that he'd done to her, but then she heard something else smash inside the apartment, and she remembered precisely why she'd left.

'I see you're still with Betriz.'

Roman nodded. 'She's amazing. So passionate.'

'You dumped Cat for her, you callous idiot,' Farah said, before something smashed through the window, sprinkling the sidewalk with plazzglass.

Roman shrugged. 'Can a firefly be blamed for seeing another light in the distance? Can a butterfly taste but one flower?'

'I need you,' Catalina said, looking up into Roman's beautiful, brown eyes and searching for some remnant of the passion he had once felt for her. Seeing nothing, she finished weakly, 'on my crew.'

'I cannot leave her,' Roman said.

'We need an Entomologist. You're the only decent one we know,' Farah said.

Roman smiled at that. 'Perhaps the hypotheses are true! Even beetles can make honey if sufficiently coaxed.'

'Damnit, Captain, I tried, but this is exactly the bullshit I'm talking about. He's got this bitch trying to kill him and he's sticking around. Forget this, forget him, he'll never listen to reason. Come on, Ken.'

Ikamon turned to go, but then spotted two men marching towards them in dark uniforms.

'Authority.'

There weren't any police in the burbdomes, not like there were on Earths 1-5, but there were definitely people who were paid to make sure everyone followed the rules. It seemed smashing one's apartment to pieces was against said rules.

'Perhaps you should go with the captain and let Betriz calm down. It would be unfortunate if the authority found your *lampyridae* and eh...evacuated it,' Ikamon said.

This, finally, seemed to knock Roman from his trance. He glanced to the pocket that now housed the firefly and then back to Catalina.

'That would be most unfortunate. I believe she is ready to lay her eggs. It would be a pity for those uncouth brutes to get their hands on her. They have no respect for the delicacy of life, you know, none at all.'

'Then come with me. We'll let Ikamon and Relkor handle them, and we'll go have a nice, quiet chat about your *lampyridae.*'

Roman nodded and Catalina grabbed his hand and led him away from the Authority.

'No, officers, we are here to *solve* the problem. It seems this poor woman is done with some loafer—we're here to pick up his things and get him outside of your fine dome,' Farah said as Catalina and Roman rounded the corner.

# 6

Once out of the sight and screams of Betriz, Roman said nothing to Catalina, only held her firmly by the hand and led her through the burbdome. The place was a maze of right angles. Sidewalks crisscrossed above and below streets that were all connected by convenience ramps and passenger ports. Nowhere did a street intersect another at anything besides a ninety-degree angle—and why should it? The entire city had been designed for efficiency. It would never need to be expanded. There would be no growth. If all went as the Corps claimed it would, nothing would have to be done to the place for the next century besides scheduled maintenance. After a time, and countless right and left turns, the gray apartment doors ended and they found themselves in a commerce sector. Now instead of rows of doors, the sidewalk was lined with rows of plazzglass windows behind which mannequins and people sat and chatted blandly. Roman led her into one of the buildings, a purported coffee shop. Much to the chagrin of her Colombian ancestors, Catalina was not a coffee snob, though her first officer was perpetually trying to turn her into one. Farah would not allow the captain to drink anything but her own heirloom varietals of coffee selected from the worlds they'd visited, hand-roasted and percolated to perfection. This place was filled with nothing of the sort.

Roman, perhaps finally noticing Catalina, withdrew his hand and mumbled an apology about how Betriz liked to come here. Immediately, Catalina missed the touch of his hand. Though the callouses and grit she'd grown to expect from his work in the field had softened, his firm, supportive grip had not. Roman had amazing hands, hands that could hold an angry scorpion at bay, or delicately put a leg band on a butterfly.

Catalina took a deep breath. These were exactly the kinds of thoughts she had to avoid if she was to recruit Roman. Catalina checked that her badges were straight in the reflection of a plazzglass display case filled with confectioneries manufactured deep in the burbdome, ordered some sort of coffee-inspired concoction for both of them, and led Roman Jupiter to an empty table.

They sat down and Catalina looked in his eyes again. She always forgot how tall Roman was. Not as tall as that amazon Betriz had been, but for a space man, 185 centimeters wasn't too shabby. He certainly towered over her scant 160. His broad chest made him look bigger still. A man chiseled from a boulder. Catalina sighed. Now was not the time.

Roman seemed to have read her mind.

'I still dream of you. Of how you looked in the captain's quarters under the light of Bubbledrive streaming through those grand windows.'

Catalina felt herself smile despite her professionalism.

'What happened to you?' Roman blurted.

There it was. That was the Roman Jupiter that Farah was always complaining about.

'I became the captain of the Institute's most advanced O-class ship.'

'O-class?' Roman's brown eyes perked up. 'I heard some of those have living libraries large enough to hold ten thousand separate specimens.'

'That's an understatement. With a good crew who understands how to build and maintain an ecological community, the *Artemis* could hold a million,' Catalina said.

'How'd you get a hold of one of those? You've been a captain, what, a couple months?'

Catalina rolled her eyes. 'It's been a year, Roman. Not all of us have been honeymooning. I was promoted after our stint on the *RL Carson.*'

'You certainly looked the part,' Roman said with his big, wicked grin.

'It was my actions that got me promoted, you pig. Badge of Valor.' Catalina tapped one of the brightly colored carbon filament badges on her dark green captain's uniform. 'The Institute found my actions above and beyond the call of duty. This planet you've been squatting on for the last year owes me its life. At least that's what it says in the record book.'

'Funny, I thought you weren't supposed to leave crew behind on Institute missions.'

Catalina glared at him. '*You* could not be found. I marked you missing and we moved on. It seems you did too.'

Roman at least had the decency to look away. 'Sola, you know how I am. Not much focus or whatever, right? But Betriz…Betriz is different. She has so much passion! I mean, you saw her back there, have you ever seen someone so filled with life?'

'She was trying to dump you.'

'Like you said, it's been a year. I think we're both trying to grow.'

'Roman, how the hell are you supposed to grow in this place?'

'I don't follow.' Roman looked absolutely confounded.

'You're an Ecologist, for the Charter's sake. Why are you stuck in this burbdome bringing in illegal flora and fauna?'

31

Roman scowled. 'This place needs some plants and bugs. To live without them is to trap the soul of man beneath one's rug. You know that, Sola.'

Catalina managed to not shudder at the awful verse of poetry. He was still writing, then. 'Of course I know that. I know that *you* know that. What I don't know is why the hell you're still here.'

'For Betriz. I couldn't possibly leave her. We're in love.'

'Roman, don't you remember Gertra, or Jenzy? You said the same thing about all of them.'

Roman shrugged. 'I know I did. It's just, I was part of a crew then, what choice did I have? It might not have lasted anyways, but Betriz, Betriz is something different. And we've been together so long. You of all people should know that a year is a lot for me, I haven't been with anyone that long since...' Roman scratched his head and thought for a moment.

'Since me, Roman. The relationship you were in before Betriz was with me. We were together for six months.'

Roman smiled that big smile of his, but his eyes filled with pain.

'And I didn't think that was going to last either, but Betriz...don't you see what we have together?' He grinned wolfishly. 'I mean, the sex alone is out of this world! Her frame and those breasts—can you believe she lifts me off the ground and shoves me into those things? It's like I'm back in zero-G.'

Catalina took a deep breath. He wasn't acting like her heart wanted him to, but this was better if he was to join her crew. Roman was over her, just like he'd gotten over every other woman he'd come across. This could work. Catalina told herself she was happy that at least she wouldn't have to be fighting off his advances anymore.

'Roman Luz Jupiter, I would like to formally extend an offer for you to serve aboard the *Artemis* as Chief Entomologist and Ensign of the Institute.'

'But, I can't leave Betriz.'

'Hear me out before you decide to stick with your biophobic girlfriend. I wouldn't come to you if I wasn't desperate. We need you. We lost our last Ecologist on an outer world to some sort of...I don't know, ground bug. Big damn things, and hungry.'

'Wait, you were on an outer world?'

'That's what I'm trying to tell you. The Institute wants to move forward with their Second Spring for the centennial. They're hoping to get the outer worlds mapped and surveyed before the Corps get out there and build more of these damn things.' Catalina gestured vaguely to the gray walls around them. 'We need *you*, Roman. We need someone of your... stamina.' Catalina gritted her teeth at the poor, but not inaccurate, word choice.

'We need someone who knows his bugs and isn't afraid to get physical. If those Corps ships had gotten to Epsilon-V before we had their drones never would have seen those monster bugs. Millions of lives could have been lost. Maybe even the whole planet. We still don't even know what those creatures were. We need you — the Institute needs you and I need you to go with us back to Epsilon-V and figure out whatever the hell those things were that got Dr. Mercurian.'

'Dr. Patrick Mercurian?'

'The one and only. You'd be filling big shoes.'

Roman nodded, seemingly lost in thought for a moment. 'Big bugs, you say? Larger than anything we've seen previously?'

'Makes a cockroach look like a house fly.'

'There were various species of roaches on the Seedpods but, regardless, that is rather interesting.'

Catalina gave him a moment to ponder before she brought out her tablet and queued up the video.

'And, Roman, you were right about the fireflies, at least on Epsilon-V.'

She passed the tablet to him and played the vid. On it, a firefly as large as her thumb crawled up her p-suit sleeve and flashed a bright yellow before flying off to join a swarm of hundreds more. Roman's eyes went wide.

'There was nothing that large on any of the Seedpods.'

'There was nothing that large in any of the known universe until we found it on Epsilon-V. Something's happening out there, Roman. All of the organisms that survived are evolving far more quickly than anyone expected. You know how on the inner worlds we find new, even novel species, but Epsilon-V was unlike anything any of us had ever seen. And that's just the first one. There's another 29 worlds that are expected to have life that are either scantly explored or completely virgin. There are probably entirely unknown ecosystems out there that have evolved from what the Institute created.'

'That we *think* we created. We certainly didn't make that firefly.'

'This is exactly the kind of thinking I need on my ship. So, will you join us?'

Roman thought about it for a long while, his broad hands rubbing his stubbly jaw, his big smile hidden behind a brooding visage. After a time, he finally looked up. His eyes were heavy with emotion. 'You understand that my heart belongs to another. My time on Bulletar has left me evolved. I lust only for Betriz now. Whatever was between us is no more, nor will it ever come to be again. I am a specialist—much like the moths of the ancient North American desert, I crave only one yucca. I don't mean to be forward, but I do not wish for you to harbor any feelings that simply cannot be returned. Much as the proboscis of said moth can never hope to sip sweet milkweed, I cannot hope to live with—'

'Yeah I get it,' Catalina said, holding up a hand to silence Roman. 'I'll be your commanding officer. It wouldn't do to fraternize with one of my ensigns.'

'It didn't stop you before,' Roman said, and his devilish grin appeared, then quickly vanished. 'Of course you have room for Betriz? She is quite a skilled violinist and can surely aide the long bouts of boredom spent in Bubbledrive.'

Catalina shook her head in disbelief. 'You really think that—' she began, but then she caught herself. 'Let me check with Farah,' she said instead and punched a few codes into her tablet, then when the response came she looked up at Roman and nodded. 'Betriz is ready for your departure.'

'Well, "to the stars" said the firefly, and the stars beckoned back.'

*'Perfecto.'* Catalina smiled.

# 7

Somehow they made it back to the port, though Catalina couldn't say how exactly. She found burbdomes supremely disorienting. Too many ninety-degree turns. In nature, no valley nor river was ever quite the same, but because the cities were painted only in shades of concrete, steel alloys, and plazzglass, each path seemed identical. Catalina was thankful when she again spotted the landing vessel of the *Artemis*, the *Arrow*. Its silhouette was something she'd fallen in love with the moment she'd seen it. Once they were back in orbit, this *Arrow* would link with others and jut out from the large half-circle that made up most of the *Artemis* and housed its biological library. Together, they looked like an arrow notched into a bow. Fitting, for a ship named after the ancient Earth goddess of the hunt. Catalina found it as she had hoped. Roman's two bags, one of which she was sure was filled with vials of insects, were loaded on the deck, and Betriz was nowhere to be seen.

'Farah!' Roman called out and waved as Catalina led him up the cargo door that—when open—served as a ramp into the side of the *Arrow*.

'It's Officer Relkor to you, Ensign. Don't forget it,' Farah said, though she was smiling.

Catalina, of course, knew why.

'I trust Ensign Jupiter's room is in order?'

'I'm sure our room will be fine, Captain, but tell me, where is the living library you boasted of? I hardly think I can show Betriz ten thousand kinds of butterfly hiding in *this*.'

'Of course not, Jupiter, this is just the sleeping quarters and landing vessel. The bulk of the *Artemis* is designed for space and will stay there unless there's reason to spend the fuel coming down to the surface. It takes time for our bacterial engines to refuel themselves and we normally can't afford that kind of time. But we always bring a few specimens we think might be useful down to the surface, in hopes of saving ourselves a trip back up. Would you like to see what we have?'

Any doubts Captain Mondragon had harbored about Roman evaporated as she watched him walk through the labeled cubes of plazzglass. 'My goodness, you found brushfoots on Texas? Where?' he'd say, then run off to another tank. 'Huh, blue crickets. From the sun, you think? Ikamon, tell me, were the fish this shade too? Fascinating. Truly fascinating. I see you brought my firefly femmes down. How interesting…considering they only eat other fireflies it's more evidence in support of my theory.'

It appeared the bait had worked well, for Roman didn't turn away from the transparent boxes of insects until the two cargo doors on the port and starboard of the cargo vessel closed shut behind the crew with a very loud and very final *clang*.

Fin had stayed up above on the *Artemis*, and Catalina didn't entirely trust computer autopilots, so she was piloting the *Arrow* when Roman realized what had happened. She felt a pang of guilt for him, if only because Farah was the only other person in the room when he inquired about his darling Betriz. Catalina had hoped she could have been the one to tell him, but of course, Farah Relkor would not be denied that opportunity.

'She's back on the planet, you dung beetle. Though she told me to tell you something. What was it? Oh yeah, "Dear Roman, you stink, don't ever come back to Bulletar. PS: I hope your flower dies." '

Roman was aghast. 'My dear Betriz? No. She has the proclivity of a damselfly when it comes to words. Surely you cannot be serious.'

Catalina could hear Ikamon shrug from her cockpit. 'It is as she says, except the flower part. She smashed that beneath her foot. *Gomenasai*.'

'I...this can't...a whole year...a year with her...I just can't...'

And with that, Roman Luz Jupiter, alleged womanizer, renowned Entomologist, and a man who by most accounts was burly, smelly, and loved getting dirty, began to cry.

# 8

The flight out of the sun's gravity well was an agonizing few days. Catalina normally relished this time of her work. It was a time of closure and of new beginnings, when one mission was over and another was yet to come. It was a time to learn about the specimens Ikamon and Farah invariably procured—a time of relaxation and refreshment. This time, however, it was none of those things, for Roman Jupiter was miserable, and he wanted the solar system to know it.

They'd already had to lock the bridge and the comm stations, for when Roman's poems of forgiveness failed to elicit a response from Betriz, he threatened to broadcast a distress call if they would not turn back. Roman now spent his days pacing through the terrariums and aquariums, staring absently at the flora and fauna within while he mumbled constantly about unrequited romance and star-crossed love.

The only thing worse than Roman's heartbreak was its effect on Farah.

'You fail to realize you've have done this to countless women on countless worlds. Look in the mirror. You'll find a cockroach.'

'If I had known they were to suffer as much as this I never would have left! I feel like the mayfly, devoid of mouth, with but one purpose: to find a lover, and yet each day I draw inextricably farther from her and closer to starvation of the soul.'

'You've left women in this state before. You left the captain like this,' Farah said, her words like crystals of ice.

'Then show me mercy by returning me to Bulletar, where at least I can hope to leave the captain without a reminder of such pain!'

'Your little hussy only exists because of Captain Mondragon. Bulletar was slated to be a whole nest of burbdomes by the Corps. Her work was the cornerstone of proving that the Institute's pledge of air, water, and sea or soil was upheld, and that the people who lived on the *actual surface* could continue to do so. It's being used as a model for all Interstellar Ecologists, which I had thought you were until we discovered you in a burbdome.'

'I am a broken man! A butterfly without a wing, ready to be returned to the food chain rather than left to turn to dust in the far reaches of the abyss.'

Catalina was impressed it never came to blows. Farah was a thin woman, but she certainly had a strength to her that could not be denied, and that coupled with her rage would probably be enough to harm even Roman's burly physique.

Ikamon tried his hand at cheering up their returned Entomologist, but he, too, had no luck. 'There are many kinds of relationships in the sea, you know. Some creatures, like whales, will mate for life. But others, like the noble squid, take many partners. I have always admired your squid-like abilities.'

'There are other creatures that, once they breed, leave their corpses for their young to consume. I had hoped the future children of Betriz and I would one day subsist off of my contributions to the universe, but I see that this crew, like hungry starfish, will slurp up what remains of my energies far before I can ever hope to return those shards of love from Betriz I had hidden away in the coral of my heart.'

This comment distracted Ikamon from his previous task of cheering up Roman and sent him rambling about the typical incompatibility of squids and coral reefs—one being exclusively shallow-water structures and the other usually being deep-dwelling denizens. Needless to say, Roman's mood did not improve.

For three days, they traveled farther and farther from Bulletar's sun, and for three days, Roman made their life a living hell. On the fourth day, they jumped to Bubbledrive.

Many believed that Bubbledrive was proof of the power of faith, because its existence demonstrated that whatever people looked for, they'd find. The classical and then neo-classical laws of physics forbade anything from traveling faster than the speed of light, and yet, somehow, human beings had found a way to reach a destination before a ray of light could. The trick, so said the physicists, was that the ships didn't actually move any faster than usual. Instead, while they cruised along as they always had, the Bubbledrive compressed space in front of them and extended space behind them, leaving the ship in a elongated sphere of seemingly normal spacetime that, while not traveling faster than the speed of light, nevertheless achieved faster-than-light results. The method had been used by the Institute to launch their Seedpods for the Great Bloom, as they sometimes tried to brand the Interstellar Spring, and was reliable enough to equip those fifty-one unmanned vessels with computer algorithms that seemed to have warped space without fail. Like so many miracles, with time it had become routine. Catalina hardly even noticed it, save for the strange colors that appeared on the edges of the bubble in which the *Artemis* was traveling. Catalina had actually been born under Bubbledrive, while traveling between two planets. With Bubbledrive, a voyage that would have taken a beam of light five years now took people ten days, and half that time was spent getting far enough away from the sun to make sure the

Bubbledrive wouldn't affect it. Some scientists were certain it wouldn't, others not so much, but everyone agreed that when compared to the thousands of years antiquated ships would have needed to cross the distances, a few days was a worthy sacrifice to prevent the possible implosion, explosion, or distortion of one of the fifty-one suns that would light the future of humanity.

Because it was still, somehow, technically impossible to transmit messages faster than light, all transmissions had to be downloaded to a ship's hard drive, then carried to a new sector where all the data could be dumped onto a planet's communications satellite, and then on to the next ship and so on, a veritable pony express though the depths of space. Because of this, transmissions between systems were virtually non-existent. Corporations had developed Bubblephone stations on asteroids deep in space that could extend a narrow path that a laser of information could be sent across, but this method was both costly and inefficient, and therefore reserved for dire emergencies and the whims of the very rich.

It was with all this in mind that Captain Mondragon responded to Fin's call from the bridge.

'Captain, the Bubblephone is flashing.'

Thinking this odd, and a bit distressing, Captain Mondragon straightened her badges of honor and went to the bridge.

'Bring it up, Ensign.'

'Yessir,' Fin said.

Captain Mondragon stiffened as the view screen came to life, but quickly deflated when nothing but a simple line of text scrolled across the screen.

'Artemis. Redirect to Wholhom, await further orders there. Direct order. Abort mission to Epsilon-V. Repeat. Redirect to Wholhom.'

Thus ended the entire message.

For a moment, Catalina did nothing save read and reread the message thrice over. No, she hadn't misread it. She was supposed to disregard Epsilon-V, the home of those horrible creatures, and go to...Wholhom? She'd never even heard of Wholhom. Well, that wasn't true, she had heard of it. Every captain worth their ship knew the name of every habitable planet, but Wholhom was a fledgling outer world, surveyed years ago. It had healthy populations of mollusks, grasses, and even honeybees. It was a colonist's dream. Why the hell was the most advanced ship the Institute had created being sent to Wholhom instead of the place that had taken a near-legendary member of its crew?

'Captain? Your orders?'

She hesitated not a moment. 'Disengage course, drop from Bubble, reconfigure course, and get us there. How long will that take?'

'Not long, Captain. A few seconds, really. We're close to Wholhom—I could practically fly there by sight.'

'No Bubbledrive, then?'

'No, sir, I mean yessir. We still need the drive, sir.'

'Fine, make it so,' Captain Mondragon said, quoting one of her favorite classic flatfilm characters. 'ETA?'

'Probably just a day in Bubble, then two or three to trek in.'

'*Perfecto.*'

# 9

The captain made every effort to maintain her composure as she left the bridge. Still, despite years developing a mask of perfect self-control, it was difficult. She couldn't respond—Bubblephones were only receivers—so she had to be content with telling herself that the Institute had a good reason for the change of assignment.

The doors to the elevator opened and Catalina found Roman there, his fist raised, his hairy knuckles about to strike the door that she had slid aside.

'Sola,' he started bashfully.

'You will address me as Captain when we are on this vessel, working planet-side on a mission, or any time you are wearing the brown-and-green uniform of the Institute for Organic Expansion or you will be confined to your quarters. At least then perhaps the rest of my crew can work in peace,' she said, squaring her shoulders against the much taller and broader figure.

Jupiter seemed to wilt under her gaze. 'Yes, err, Captain, that's why I wanted to talk to you. I think that perhaps I was a bit hasty in trying to sabotage your mission. I should not have tried to send a distress beacon back to Bulletar.'

'You will never be able to do anything with my systems that I don't know about, *Ensign*. You may know bugs, but I know this ship. Don't ever think you can do so much as pluck a flower without my permission or knowledge,' Catalina said, and Roman wilted further.

'Yes, well, good, then. I had noticed we had dropped out of Bubbledrive and was hoping that it wasn't on account of me.'

Catalina actually laughed at that. 'Ha! You think I was going to stop because you shed a few tears? Grow up, Jupiter. I knew you were going to get over her, just like you got over every other girl that either begged you to stay or begged you to leave. You have the attention span of one of your fireflies, and if it wasn't for your ability to understand the things, I wouldn't have you on my ship. If you think for a moment that I am doing anything besides what is expressly best for this mission and the Charter, you are a far bigger fool than even Farah takes you for.'

'Then why did we drop out of Bubbledrive?' Roman said, struggling to maintain eye contact with this short and powerful post of a woman.

'Because of the *mission*. Get to the mess hall. I have an announcement for the crew.'

'You mean Farah and Ikamon?'

'Shut up and steady yourself. We're about to go back under Bubble. You've been a groundworm for a year. I don't want you getting sick. '

Catalina felt the slightest of tremors as space stretched out in both directions, yet also in opposite dimensions. Roman somehow managed to fall into Catalina's arms. She caught him easily. It wouldn't do for a small woman to not know how to defend herself against a larger man's body. She carried his momentum to the floor and managed to not crack his head against the deck, much as she might have wanted to.

Jupiter's eyes opened and he swooned. In his eyes was something that Catalina had told herself she did not want to see again, a look she had seen far too many times before.

'Sola, I've been a fool!' His eyelashes fluttered like one of the butterflies he was always going on about.

'You will address me as Captain,' Catalina said, and then dropped Roman. This time, his head hit the deck with a satisfying clunk.

'Yes, Captain, anything you say!' Roman hopped up and saluted. 'Coccinellidae! I've been a fool, a bumblebee searching for a rose when all the while a marigold, far brighter and richer in nutrients, is right in front of me.'

Catalina didn't know what to say to that, so she ignored him.

'Mess hall. Now.'

Roman winked, saluted again, more crisply this time, and marched off.

Catalina couldn't be sure, but she thought he might've been sucking in his gut as he went.

# 10

Captain Mondragon was beginning to regret crewing the *Artemis* with old friends—Farah Relkor seemed to have given up completely on decorum.

'This has got to be a joke! The *Artemis* went to Epsilon-V *first*, we have surveys to complete, and what's more we lost a man there. A good one too. Please take offense, Jupiter.'

'Captain, we should ask for clarification in this matter, you know? It is highly unorthodox to be reassigned,' Ikamon said.

Only Roman seemed supportive, and that, too, was infuriating.

'Don't you think that Sola, pardon me, Captain Sola has considered all of this? She would not leave a survey uncompleted and a man behind unless the Institute gave her good reason for it. She is an asset to the Institute for Organic Expansion. I mean, just look at her badges, there's like ten more since I last saw her, and it's only been a year. I can't even imagine taking off that jacket any more, there'd be far too much risk of bruising her firm but supple skin.'

'Roman, that is enough!' Catalina said, but Roman only grinned.

Farah rolled her eyes. 'Shouldn't use the captain's middle name, Ensign. Remember you're ranked below deck scrubber now. It's unprofessional to use anything but titles.' When Farah said this she looked pointedly at Catalina. Clearly she noticed that Catalina had called Roman by his first name, but how could she not? He was fawning all over her like they were back in the captain's quarters on the *RL Carson* under Bubbledrive with nothing to do but each other. She stole a glance out one of the ports and saw the strange aurora of lights flashing by as the *Artemis* traveled on towards Wholhom.

'Ensign Jupiter has a good point,' Ikamon began, before Farah turned on him, her pale eyes were aflame. Ikamon held up his hands in protest. 'The captain would not change missions unless the Institute gave her good reason. This is, after all, unprecedented. We must hear her out.'

Farah crossed her arms and scowled but said nothing more.

Three pairs of eyes fell upon Catalina.

Catalina was unsure of how to tell them that the Institute hadn't told her a damn thing, that all they had said was that the mission had changed. She'd never been reassigned like this before—so far as she knew no one had, but then no one had ever faced anything like the strange, giant bugs they'd seen on Epsilon-V, either. Before she could speak, Fin's voice crackled over the comm system.

'Do you just want me to read them the message, Captain?'

Catalina interjected before Farah exploded.

'That won't be necessary, pilot, I believe I remember what it said.' Catalina cleared her throat. '*Artemis*. Redirect to Wholhom, await further orders there. Direct order. Abort mission to Epsilon-V. Repeat. Redirect to Wholhom.'

Roman nodded in understanding and appreciation. Farah cocked her head, clearly unsure of what to think. Only Kensei said anything. 'But what is the message?'

'That is the message,' Catalina said flatly.

Roman spoke first. 'I, for one, find it commendable that we are following the orders of the Institute and heading to Wholhom—an inner planet, certainly, but surely a world in need of our assistance to establish the networks of life we all find so dear. I find it respectable and, in truth, quite attractive that Captain Sola holds the Institute in such regard—'

To her credit, Farah didn't yell when she silenced Roman's inane blathering. Her tone of voice was fearsome enough to stop him. 'That's it? That's all they told you and now we're supposed to leave a man's corpse, and a whole planet, to what? Rot?'

'My Mango, we cannot possibly know what they plan to do,' Ikamon said.

'What I *know* is that we are owed far more of an explanation than *that*. This is the first planet we've ever encountered hostile life on, and we are being reassigned without so much as a mention of what is going to become of that world?' Farah said.

'Bubblephone is expensive, I'm sure they'd have told us more if they could afford to,' Jupiter said.

'If they could afford to? They started life on the 51 Seeded Worlds, you unevolved biped, of course they can afford it! We have a duty to uphold! We have to prove that each planet has air, water, and sea or soil in the few years we still have before the Corps comes in and drops prefabs on everything the Institute has created, everything we've been studying. We can't just abandon our mission!'

'We are not abandoning our mission, Officer Relkor,' Catalina said.

'Sir, with all due respect, my surveys are incomplete, as are Ken's.'

'I am fully aware of the status of your reports. As aware as you must be of how I feel about insubordination on this ship. I have had quite enough of your outbursts. I understand that this is unprecedented, and I, too, feel slighted that we are being reassigned and that our duty to Epsilon-V is going to be fulfilled by what I am sure will be an inferior crew, but if you want to whine and throw a tantrum about it, why not just come over here and cry into my tits.'

'Captain, I am feeling quite a bit of emotional distress over our reassignment.'

'Shut up Jupiter!' Kensei, Farah and Catalina all yelled at once. Fin chuckled over the intercom.

'Now, if you think you have the fortitude to skip all this nonsense about your bruised ego and hurt feelings, I would like to remind you of our vows to uphold the Charter. We swore no oath to Epsilon-V, nor did we swear any oath to Dr. Mercurian. Our duty lies with the Charter alone. More than ninety years ago, the Institute sent out the 51 Seedpods into the vastness of space because they hoped that one day each planet would have breathable air, drinkable water, and either tillable soil or fishable seas. They did this when humanity was poised on environmental collapse because we were simply *out of space*. These worlds represent the ultimate solution to this problem, yet they cannot be inhabited until we prove them to be safe. We owe nothing to Epsilon-V. Nor does the Institute owe us a hug and a "sorry-about-your-loss," for the death of Patrick. We have pledged ourselves to the Institute and the Charter they created because of what we owe *them*. I have stepped onto thirteen worlds, and now the Institute is telling us to go to a fourteenth, because they, or it—or at the very least some bureaucrat working there who is hopefully less emotional than the three of you—knows that the *Artemis* is a strong ship with a strong crew. I hope, as I'm sure you all do, that when we drop from Bubbledrive there will be a full report on what will happen to Epsilon-V until we get there, but if we do not find such a report encoded and waiting for us on the databank of a comm satellite, you can be sure that I will not call up the Institute and yell at them about it.

'Instead, we will read whatever report that Institute will undoubtedly have on Wholhom, survey the state of the organisms the Institute seeded it with, ascertain if the planet has air, water, and soil or sea, and if it does not, we will solve this problem or else the Corps will come in and drop a burbdome on this planet and take away whatever chance the colonists have to live as human beings. We will complete our mission, protect this planet, and give humanity another world on which they may continue to live. We will do this as we always have, efficiently and with great care. Just because a few members of the old crew from the *RL Carson* are back together does not give any one of us reason to pretend like we can still behave like we did back then, back before I was one of the most decorated officers in the Institute, and your captain. Now, if there's to be any more objections, kindly write them in your ship's logs. I have heard quite enough for today. Questions? No? *Perfecto.*'

Farah, Ikamon, and Roman stood eyes wide and silent, until a loud clap ran over the comm systems, then another, and another, faster and faster. Captain Mondragon and Roman realized that Fin was giving the captain a slow clap over the intercom, but only Roman found it appropriate to clap along with her.

'Pilot Fin, do I need autopilot to take us the rest of the way to Wholhom?'

'No, Captain,' Fin said. The clapping stopped.

'Captain, if I may,' Roman said his big grin growing bigger by the second.

'No, you may not, Ensign Jupiter. I don't want to hear a word from any of you until we drop out of Bubbledrive in two days. Is that clear?'

Farah Relkor, Kensei 'Ikamon' Mizuyama, and Roman Luz Jupiter all saluted and barked, 'Yes, sir!'

Captain Mondragon left the bridge knowing full well that two days of silence was far too much to ask from a crew as special as hers.

# 11

To his credit, Roman lasted nearly a day. After the way he'd been eyeing her, Catalina had expected him to come knocking on her door far sooner. So when he did rap his hairy knuckles against her quarters, she was not surprised. She did peep through her window before opening the door, and she was glad she did, for it gave her a moment to regain her composure.

Roman had brought her butterflies.

Catalina had a weakness for flowers. She was a captain of an O-class ship, after all, and had a certain affinity for life in all of its forms. Flowers especially, she loved. They were colorful and aromatic and all that was great, of course, but what she loved most about them was that in each head of almost every flower, there were hundreds, if not thousands of little versions of that flower, each waiting to spring forth and grow into another beautiful version intent on making even more of itself. She loved the asters most of all, for they were all composite flowers, and positively overflowed with seeds between their petals.

Roman, it seemed, had remembered this detail, but had gone one step further. In his hairy knuckles he clutched a bouquet of dwarf sunflowers, blackfoot daisies, *damianita*, and zinnias, asters one and all, and no doubt picked from Farah's terrariums housed in the living library of the ship without her permission. What was even more impressive, though, and a trick only Roman in all his romantic obnoxiousness was capable of, was that three pipevine swallowtail butterflies fluttered lazily about the bouquet, pausing to sip nectar now and then, or land upon Roman's shoulder and flap their blue-black iridescent wings languidly. Between the flowers and the butterflies was Roman Jupiter. He was freshly shaved, his short, unruly hair was slicked back into some semblance of a professional appearance, and he wore a spotless uniform.

Catalina took a deep breath, reminded herself that Roman was a great Entomologist but a terrible boyfriend, and opened the door.

'Ensign, I believe my orders were clear.'

Roman nodded and gently thrust the flowers in her direction. Catalina only glared at Roman at first, but when one of the butterflies fluttered between them, she snatched the flowers out of Roman's hands. Roman looked at her but said nothing as the three pipevine swallowtails followed the bouquet into her room. Catalina knew that as soon as she closed the door the butterflies would stop behaving as if they were tame, but so long as Roman was around, they'd dote on her. She didn't know how he did things like this with insects — whether it was pheromones or perhaps conditioning imposed as soon as they hatched from a chrysalis — but it was intoxicating nonetheless. A butterfly landed on one of her brightly colored badges of honor that was in the shape of a lily, its delicate frame so small that it didn't so much as nudge the pin a degree askew.

'What do you want, Jupiter?'

Roman mimed zipping his lips and winked at Catalina.

'You came here to tell me you destroyed some of Farah's breeding stock and are in the process of murdering the only swallowtails we got from Texas? If that is all, you are dismissed.'

Roman bowed cordially and smiled again.

Catalina closed the door. Part of her wanted to toss the flowers into the composter, but they were beautiful, and besides, the butterflies would need something to eat. One of them nibbled at a daisy now, its delicate proboscis carefully uncurling and drinking the nectar. Catalina sighed and fetched a pitcher and some water. She placed the flowers into the pitcher and noticed that in the middle of the bouquet was a rolled-up paper note. She smirked. She knew that Roman had more planned than simply being nice. It seemed Farah was right. He was still his old self, regardless of how he'd behaved with Betriz. She unfurled the note and read the words written upon it.

*Dearest Captain Sola,*

*Forgive me for my earlier intrusions against both your loyalty to the Charter and your professionalism. I see now how obvious it was that Betriz needed to stay behind on Bulletar. Honestly, I don't know what I saw in her, and would like to thank you for getting me back in space, and reminding me of the work we used to do together.*

*Much has changed in a year, Captain. Even writing that word is new for me. I still remember you as that meteoric first officer of the RL Carson, highly decorated, intelligent, intimidating, passionate beyond measure, and outstandingly beautiful. I believe it is these feelings, perhaps, that offended you, and for these feelings I would like to explain myself and apologize. You see, when I saw you under the light of the Bubbledrive, I felt as if I had a flashback to the firm mattress of your quarters on the Carson. I felt as if my neck was bruised from your love bites, my loins tired from your formidable sexual prowess. I remembered the way the light used to dance upon your naked thighs, the way your long, curly hair would flow around us when you turned off the gravity, the way your eyes would sparkle when you'd look at me like I was one of those planets we'd be seeing as soon as we dropped from Bubbledrive. I still lust for you at night when I sleep. I wake up aching, thinking of the dancing lights and the things you would do to me, the things we'd do to each other. I never imagined that that beautiful, capable woman would turn from first officer acting as a captain in time of emergency to Captain of her own ship in hardly a year and come find me, of all people. I would say it is an honor, but in truth it is so much more than that. I feel like the butterfly, left behind during the great migration only to discover that another of his own has returned for him, if only to mate and leave their fertilized offspring on the underside of a dewy leaf.*

*I know that we are not butterflies and that we cannot go back to those wonderful, unforgettable moments that I relive every time I see the flickering aurora of faster-than-light travel, those lights that you were born under. Perhaps I should take to thanking those lights for watching over a woman as amazing as you come into existence, for without them you may have never come to be. If that was so then the universe would be a drab place indeed, because without you my most treasured memories would be nothing but erotic fantasies about a perfect woman. I'm thankful for those moments and recognize that they are locked in our memories forever, and that we cannot hope to re-create them, no matter how much we might want to, for time has passed, and that part of us is gone.*

*You are my captain now, and I am yours to do with as you wish. I want you to understand that I understand all that passion is behind us, and that I will do my best to ignore such lustful memories whenever I am in your presence. It may take some time, but I am committed to respecting the captain you have become, and will do my best to behave as one of the admirable people you have crewed.*

*Respectfully and forever yours, Roman Luz Jupiter*

*P.S. those flowers needed to be thinned and the swallowtails already laid clutches of eggs and will probably die in a few days. I thought that it would be better to let them appreciate your presence than die without beholding the being to whom they owe their life, much as you have given me the same opportunity. But I digress. Rest assured I will always—*

From there it seemed as though something had been crossed out repeatedly. Catalina considered trying to uncover what Roman had worked so hard to hide, but figuring it was probably just another ruse, she crumpled up the poorly veiled love note and threw it in the composter.

She knew what Roman was doing, and love note or not, he was not going to rekindle what they once had.

Catalina Mondragon pushed the letter from her mind, told herself Roman was only trying to relive his glory days, and stood up to go to the bridge to check on their ETA to Wholhom. It was difficult to ignore how wet her panties had become from reading the note, yet if anyone could do it, it was undoubtedly the captain of the *Artemis*.

# 12

The drop from Bubbledrive was far less remarkable than being in it. The stars didn't cease to blur like they did in old flatfilms, nor was there any feeling of a shift in motion. All that happened was that the aurora of multicolored lights around the *Artemis* ceased to be, and there in the distance in front of the ship, a star burned far brighter than the others. Gliese 777, it had been named by the Earth-stuck astronomers who'd first noticed it. Now, it was simply referred to as Wholhom. Few systems had more than one habitable planet orbiting a star, and people tended to care little for things they couldn't touch or stand upon. It was possible that the people of Wholhom had given their star a name, as Earth's Sun was called Sol, but if they had, few probably knew the name and even fewer cared to use it.

Catalina noticed the star as happenstance. Her attention was focused on the planet itself; Wholhom could be seen off to the port side of the star. Fin hadn't come in at the best possible distance—that would have put the planet directly between them and the sun—but given the last-minute readjustments, the captain was sure Fin had calculated the most efficient course and found that trekking in under thrusters was a quicker alternative than spiraling around the gravitational wells of the sun and planets to get a bit closer.

'ETA?'

'Three days Captain. It would be less, but I figured we should drop out to confirm orders, and the difference only amounts to a few hours. Actually, based on the other gas giants in orbit, I have an interesting hypothesis on how we can leave and shorten our time out of Bubble,' Fin said, but Catalina wasn't really listening. The reports were coming in, filling their databanks with information expressed in words, pictures, and videos from their friends and loved ones across the inhabited sector of the galaxy, as well as business proposals, advertisements, and digital piles of junk mail. Catalina didn't care for any of that. She only wanted a report from the Institute on their orders and the state of Epsilon-V.

'Captain, I see nothing carrying the Institute's data stamp.'

'Their encryption often costs them speed. We should be receiving their transmission in the next hour or so.'

'Do you want any of this other stuff?'

'Tell Wholhom the *Artemis* is here and en route to bring them air, water, and soil or sea in three days. We'll need a full briefing, a liaison, and landing clearance as near to the epicenter of whatever ecological emergency is so important that we needed to come here instead of Epsilon-V,' Catalina took a deep breath. 'Not that last part, of course, Pilot.'

'Of course, Captain,' Fin said and hastily deleted a few key strokes as her round cheeks turned red beneath her pink hair.

They needed to purchase very little on the *Artemis*. Equipped with the organic output of the composters, Farah and Ikamon could grow more than enough food for their meager crew. They didn't need fuel, for the bacterial fuel cells of the *Artemis* would be fully charged from the light of Wholhom's sun by the time they reached Wholhom. 3D printers could make any tools they'd need, an autoloom could handle clothing, and the ship had a repair bay to maintain the drones that went about its hallways fixing the vessel. Few people wrote letters to any of the crew of the *Artemis*. A life in deep space and planet hopping didn't make much for permanent contacts, though, it seemed Roman had somehow gotten his forwarding address out and a few private messages appeared in the queue for him. Catalina briefly considered giving them a look—she had full rights to any information, personal or otherwise, on her ship—but she forwarded them on without opening them. It wasn't really her business who Roman was talking with, even if he had spent the last few days attempting to woo her.

It hadn't seemed to Farah or Ikamon that that was what Roman was doing, but Catalina knew better. Roman had used their time under Bubble to familiarize himself with what insects the late Dr. Mercurian had collected and that the crew of the *Artemis* had managed to keep alive without an Entomologist. He also cleaned empty cages, reorganized the data base of insects, and cross-referenced Farah's biomes of plants and fungus with his new system. When he wasn't busy with that, he organized the cargo hold, inspected the central composter, and generally just tidied up. While he did all this, he didn't say a word.

'What the hell did you do to him, Captain?' Farah asked, her smile wide, eyes gleaming.

'I told him to not talk to me while we were under Bubbledrive. He followed my orders.'

Farah had rolled her eyes, but Catalina suspected that she was impressed. As far as Catalina knew, nothing with two legs had ever gotten Roman to be quiet without having sex with him and waiting for him to fall asleep first.

Ikamon had also approached her about Roman's behavior, though his concerns were the opposite of his wife's. 'Captain, I believe Roman is not feeling well. All he does is work. He is not like his old self, you know?'

'He's probably making up for the last year wasted,' Catalina replied.

'Mm...*eto*, perhaps I can spend some time off-duty with him?'

'I see nothing wrong with that. Just keep it off the bridge.'

Ikamon saluted and went off, but he came back to her the next day, just as dejected. 'I do not understand him. We drank a few beers like old times and tried to talk, but he would not. He seemed very interested in the aquatic insects we found on Graken, but he did not say a word.'

'At least someone on this dirt bucket knows how to follow orders.'

Ikamon had said nothing to that, only widened his eyes and saluted.

But Catalina knew what Roman was doing. The bastard was trying to win her over. He was trying to prove he was a new man. He knew what his letter and his butterflies would do to her, and by not speaking while he worked he was demonstrating that he could follow his captain's orders down to the letter. He was doing his job efficiently, improving morale on the ship—Farah's emotional temperament far outweighed her husband's as far as the overall atmosphere of the *Artemis* was concerned—and he was doing it all with a smile. The bastard even apologized in his letter for still thinking she was beautiful, or something along those lines. Catalina found herself regretting that she had composted the letter, and was apprehensive that Roman, in his newfound interest in ship systems and cleanliness, might have found it in the bowels of the ship. If he did, it didn't so much as put a chip in his grin. All and all, he seemed to be a more professional, kinder, and better man than the one Catalina had left behind on Bulletar for someone taller and with far larger breasts than hers. If it wasn't for one trifling detail, Catalina might have been naive enough to think he had changed. But Roman had forgotten all about Betriz. He was the same as he'd ever been. He chased a new woman on every planet he ever set foot on, and yet he was strangely patient and had always been skilled at the long game. Despite knowing all this, despite having seen Roman do the same thing a dozen times on the *RL Carson* before they got together, Catalina still found herself attracted to him. There was just something about him. Maybe it was his confidence, or his broad, hairy chest. Maybe it was his aggressive though not necessarily unpleasant musk, or the way he babbled in poorly constructed naturalist poetry. Most likely, though, it was the way he looked at her, his eyes crawling all over her skin as they followed the eddies and flows of the lights of the Bubbledrive, that Catalina found so difficult to resist.

'Incoming, Captain. It seems the Institute has decided to grace us with their orders,' Fin pulled Catalina from her thoughts.

'Watch the tone, pilot.'

'Aye, Captain,' Fin said.

Catalina had full confidence that her own smirk was completely internal.

'Captain Catalina Solaris Xao Mondragon, I am General Ecologist Boris Aprocrita,' the General Ecologist's voice boomed from the telescreen, not butchering a single one of Catalina's multitude of names. Catalina didn't recognize the face or the name, just his rank. The man hadn't seen a lot of planets by the look of badges he sported on his coat—Catalina had more accolades than he—but his rank was of General, which meant he helped oversee the entire galactic ecosystem. He was more than the captain of a ship that merely collected specimens from a single planet at a time. Catalina saluted the video and listened with intent.

'Wholhom is experiencing a crisis we expect the *Artemis* is best equipped to solve. It seems the chief crop of Wholhom, *Arachis hypogaea*, is undergoing unexpected and terminal failure, and has been for a few standards. The colonists will not likely survive the volatile climate of the planet without it.

Thank you for your prompt handling of this task. Your acquisition and demotion of Ensign Roman Luz Jupiter is noted. Once your task is complete on Wholhom you will bring him to Earth-1 for debriefing. That will be all. We all must grow for the Charter,' the General Ecologist said.

'The Charter grows because of us,' Captain Mondragon replied and saluted.

With that, the screen went back to the view of Wholhom and its sun twinkling in the distance, having grown in size not at all since they saw it but a few seconds ago.

'Captain? Is that it?'

'Pilot?'

'Is there not an encoded message of some kind? A secret mission?' Fin asked.

'No, Fin.'

Fin furrowed her brow. 'Captain, why didn't he mention what is happening on Epsilon-V?'

'It is unlikely General Ecologist Apocrita is familiar with the particulars of every mission ever run on every ship.'

Fin laughed, a single, big, loud guffaw, but when Catalina said nothing, the young pilot turned to face the captain with a look of horror. 'Captain Mondragon, is there something I don't understand? Why are we being demoted to some bunk mission helping farmers on a planet with safe but bland life that's been surveyed before, and why do they want to debrief Jupiter and not us? Epsilon-V was the craziest place I've ever seen!' Something dawned on Fin and her face lit up. She straightened her hunched posture and smiled winningly at Catalina. 'Sir, pardon my ignorance. I heard *crops* and failed to realize the possible significance, sir.'

'What are you talking about?'

'Sir, I have a confession. I might have lied on my resume.'

'Might have?'

'I sort of exaggerated some things I've done, not lied exactly. I would've told you sooner but it's just that I had to make sure you'd keep me on the ship and respect me for the skills that I had and that you needed, and *not* the skills you *thought* you needed.'

'You've more than proven your abilities to handle the *Artemis*, and I didn't believe for a second that you could do all those maneuvers you listed anyway.'

'Sir, I did those maneuvers. Set the textbook vid for some of them too.'

'Then what on Earth-1 are you blabbering about?' Catalina said, wiping the grin off of Fin's face.

'I didn't get straight A's in ecology. I can tell the bugs mostly. I mean, I know what a butterfly is, the fish are easy, and the mollusks are pretty different, but I uh…I don't know my plants, sir. I had to beg the professor to pass me. What is uh…' Fin took a deep breath, '*Arachis hypogaea?*'

Catalina sighed, she knew her pilot's resume had been too good to be true. No one knew how to fly like Fin did, fix a ship, *and* Interstellar Ecology. At least the poor thing had pronounced the Latin correctly.

'Peanuts, Fin, they want us to help farm peanuts.'

# 13

Dr. La'Shay Winston had never seen an O-class ship until the *Artemis* entered the orbit of Wholhom. She watched through the polished lenses of a locally made telescope, admiring the graceful curves of the organic starship. The long, thin prow and massive half-circle that Winston knew comprised the living library that made the O-class ships so famous resembled an arrow notched into a bow, but as it adjusted in flight, La'Shay Winston saw it was a far more seductive craft than that. Large flanges, invisible from below, gave a feminine and feline cast to the silhouette of the ship, like a cat's haunches tightly coiled and ready to strike. With an almost invisible puff of jets, the long prow on the front of the ship detached, like an arrow firing from a bow, then broke into several pieces that descended into Wholhom's atmosphere.

Ships on Wholhom had none of its grace. Most were boxy freighters, few even capable of interstellar travel. Wholhom was one of the closest outer planets, or farthest inner planets, depending on one's perspective. It had a healthy ecological system, complete with soil bacteria, algae, fungus, and a fair amount of grasses and annual wildflowers. The briny sea was populated with mollusks, and Wholhom was even lucky enough to have honeybees. All in all, it probably would have been considered an inner planet if it had been settled but a few years earlier, and if Dr. La'Shay Winston hadn't needed to call the Institute to save her people from starvation.

Dr. Winston tried to hold her head high as the shuttle of the *Artemis* completed its landing sequence. A large hatch opened on the underside of the vessel and out she came, the near-legendary Captain, Catalina Solaris Xao Mondragon. Only once had she failed the Charter—countless other times she had solved problems where no one else could, where it had seemed the only viable option was to give up on the ecology of an entire planet for life inside a Corporate burbdome. La'Shay prayed that the captain and her crew would be able to help Wholhom as they had helped so many other planets before.

Captain Mondragon marched towards La'Shay, her gait even crisper than her perfect uniform. Her badges of honor, arranged on her breast in perfect rows, twinkled in the blueish light of Wholhom's sun. She was shorter than La'Shay had pictured, but was as perfectly groomed as her reputation. La'Shay immediately regretted not wearing a clean lab coat. She made little time to clean her white coveralls, and for the Wholhom farming community, grit was respect. Dr. Winston was respected by some of the gruffer farmers instead of only tolerated, because they knew that she wasn't afraid to collect her own samples and that she knew her way around an Ultra-Reaper. Of course La'Shay couldn't expect the captain of a worlds-renowned O-class ship from the Institute to follow the same code of conduct. Her heart pounded even faster when she saw the crew of the *Artemis* emerge behind the captain. None of them carried the same prestige as Captain Mondragon, but La'Shay hoped to learn much from Farah Relkor and had arranged for Julia Tartren to escort the enigmatic Ikamon to Wholhom's salty seas to glean what knowledge she could from the Marine Biologist. La'Shay had to remove her glasses and clean them when she saw the third member of the crew. She had expected to see Dr. Patrick Mercurian, an Entomologist nearly as renowned as Captain Mondragon, but instead of the geriatric doctor, a brute of a man walked toward her. La'Shay put her glasses back on and saw that his uniform—though just as clean as the others—only carried the rank of ensign, and had no badges of honor to add to his credibility. Of the four of them, only the ensign smiled, a wide, roguish grin that shone out beneath his strong nose. La'Shay might have found him attractive if it wasn't for the hair sprouting from his neck and knuckles.

'We all must grow for the Charter,' La'Shay saluted.

'The Charter grows because of us,' Captain Mondragon saluted back. 'I take it you are the planet's Botanist, Dr. La'Shay Winston?'

'Yes, Captain Mondragon, and may I just say it is an honor to meet you. I have followed your career through the comms and I wanted to say how excited I was when I heard that you got the *Artemis* and the crew you selected. I mean, Dr. Relkor and Mr. Ikamon are legends in their own right, and Dr. Mercurian—'

'Is no longer with us,' Captain Mondragon interrupted.

La'Shay felt her confidence slip. She only hoped she appeared to have the captain's resolve. 'I had hoped your crew and Dr. Mercurian could help us.' She removed her glasses and polished them absentmindedly on her labcoat. 'We have a beetle problem and our planetary Entomologist is a specialist in honeybees. The best in the inhabited sector, in fact, but he's the first to admit he doesn't know much else. Because of the early reports on the health of Wholhom, the Institute didn't see a reason to send people that could be better needed elsewhere. I have learned much about how to care for this world, but we had hoped that Dr. Mercurian and Dr. Relkor could—'

Again, Captain Mondragon cut her off. 'You will find the talents of our Entomologist more than adequate for farming peanuts. Now, if you would kindly dispense with the pleasantries, we need to get down to business. Every minute wasted on Wholhom is a minute not spent investigating Epsilon-V and what happened to the eminent doctor.'

'I—I'm sorry?' La'Shay said.

'Surely you watch the holos? Dr. Mercurian is dead,' Farah Relkor said. If she noticed what the harshness of her words did to La'Shay, she did not seem to care. 'Patrick died on Epsilon-V months ago. We were en route there when the Institute sent us here because you weren't handling your end of the Charter. Wholhom's initial surveys indicated that this planet had a good variety of life and that most of your flora has adapted well to the spectrum of your sun. Rumor is, you even have honeybees. Should be a walk in the park to farm this planet. What happened?'

La'Shay's mouth worked dumbly, but before she could find it in herself to form anything useful to say, the Entomologist spoke up. 'Captain, if I may ask her a question?' Captain Mondragon nodded. The Entomologist smiled and looked at La'Shay, his brown eyes sinking into her darker ones. 'Ensign Roman Luz Jupiter, at your service, madam, and I assure you, though I lack the honors and esteem of my colleagues, I will do everything in my power to make your life here on Wholhom a better one. What, may I ask, is that charming device you are wearing that ever-so-slightly magnifies your eyes and makes them positively sparkle?'

La'Shay found herself talking without even thinking. 'You've never seen glasses?' she said, again removing them and cleaning them on her coat.

The man Jupiter shook his head no.

'Oh damn it, here we go,' Dr. Relkor said, only adding to La'Shay's confusion.

'We don't have surgical facilities on Wholhom yet, so the glassworkers at our telescope shop polished me corrective lenses. I can't see a thing without them, well, nothing small anyway.'

'*Them?*' Jupiter said, as if testing the pronoun. Finding it to his liking he continued, 'well, *they* are absolutely spectacular, and I hate to say that I hope your planet never achieves the technological prowess to take away those charming devices from your beautiful face. What they do to your cheekbones is simply astounding. It reminds me of the beauty of a skipper butterfly emerging from its chrysalis, for you see, the chrysalis only heightens the beauty of the—'

'That will be quite enough, Ensign. We have work to do,' Captain Mondragon said and Roman Jupiter snapped to attention. La'Shay found herself strangely pleased to see that Jupiter's wide smile did not leave his face entirely.

# 14

'So you see that's why I'd hoped for the expertise of Dr. Mercurian,' La'Shay finished, lamely.

Catalina nodded. She wished that Patrick was here as well. As it happened, she had sent Roman to go wander the fields while she and Farah spoke with La'Shay for fear of the Entomologist beguiling the already frazzled doctor.

'So let me get this straight,' Farah said, pushing back her straight, blonde hair and taking a deep breath. 'The peanuts weren't producing food or fixing nitrogen anywhere close to spec, and some were even depleting your soil of what nitrogen had accumulated since the Institute's Seedpod got here, what, sixty-eight standards ago?'

La'Shay nodded. Farah didn't slow down enough to notice.

'You noticed there were little black beetles everywhere, so you tried to manage for them. Organics weren't working, so you tried pesticides. Those worked for a year and the peanuts got better, but then the beetles came back and the peanuts did worse than ever. After that, you tried the dangerously outdated strategy of expanding your peanut farmland so the beetles wouldn't have a habitat to stay in.'

'We have beekeepers who bring in the pollinators,' La'Shay started, 'so there shouldn't be any pests. None were on the Seedpods and no one had introduced them. It's just these beetles—' Farah held up a hand and La'Shay's strength left her. Catalina felt bad for the woman. Here she was, meeting two of her heroes in the flesh, and they were bullying her. Catalina told herself she'd go nicer on the groundworm. Farah didn't seem to find this a priority.

'You tried the rather absurd strategy of planting only peanuts and, by some stroke of dumb luck, that worked—or did for a while, anyway—and that's what got us to this.' Farah gestured to the peanut fields around them. They stretched on for kilometers, past the horizon, as far as they could see. They'd driven into the field on an Ultra-Reaper, but after what seemed an eternity of traversing row after row of peanuts, the captain had ordered La'Shay to stop. La'Shay had mumbled something about the mountains not being much farther, but Farah had silenced her with a glare.

'So then what happened? The beetles came back?' Farah asked.

'No, but the peanuts are doing worse than ever.' La'Shay knelt down and pulled one of the peanut plants out from the soil. It was tiny and poorly formed and the few peanuts it had produced were shrunken.

'Well its nodes look good,' Farah said, gently touching the red lumps attached to the roots of the plants, 'and you certainly have a healthy fungus population.'

'Yes, we've always been lucky with that. Even now, with the beetles gone and the peanuts dying, the mycelium seem strong as ever,' La'Shay said.

'Officer Relker, I don't understand. I'm familiar with mycelium, the underground parts of mushrooms that compose the real bulk of the organism, but what on Earth-1 is a node?' Captain Mondragon asked the Botanist.

'A node is the part of the peanut plant that houses the bacteria that takes nitrogen from the air and fixes it into a form that can be used by plants in the soil. Normally, in a crop of legumes like peanuts it's the first thing I check. If the nodes are green, grey, or white instead of pinkish or red, it's a good indicator that the crop hasn't been properly inoculated, but that is not the case here. These seem healthy, and the plants are definitely interfacing with the fungus—the nodes have more mycelium attached than I've ever seen.'

'Could it be that the nodes on this planet have a different color that indicates health?' the captain said.

'No, ma'am. We brought the peanuts with us from Earth-4, and we monitor them extensively. They haven't even evolved into a distinct species yet,' La'Shay said.

Catalina took a deep breath, ready to let it go, but Farah couldn't help herself. 'The proper salute for a captain is *sir*, not *ma'am*.'

La'Shay looked confused. 'I thought that since you were a woman—'

'That you should treat us differently? Rank has nothing to do with gender, *Doctor*, not at the Institute, not anymore. I thought you said you had followed our exploits,' Farah said.

'I—I look up to you *because* you are women,' La'Shay stammered.

'Our gender has nothing to do with our abilities. It's that kind of thinking that kept women off of the first spaceships,' Farah said, her voice growing hot.

'I didn't mean anything—'

'The proper salute is *sir*. Do you understand, Doctor?' Catalina said, keeping her voice emotionless.

'Yes...sir. I just thought—'

'Would you prefer us to call you Miss Winston instead of Doctor?' Farah said.

'No! Of course not. I apologize, I didn't know.'

'Now you do. What about the fungi, are they providing nutrients?' Catalina said, hoping to redirect the conversation.

'Yes...sir,' La'Shay said, 'we did an extensive survey a few standards ago, before all this got bad. They transport nitrogen, sugar, and a mix of necessary minerals and nutrients to and from the plant. They're doing well with the peanuts. Better than they did when this area was still wildflowers and grasses, actually.'

'Curious,' Farah said.

Catalina didn't press her. She knew Farah well enough to be sure that if she had more to her hypothesis, she would say so.

'I only have one more question for you, Doctor. What could have possibly compelled you to plant so many peanuts?' Catalina asked.

La'Shay tried to smile, but ended up only removing her glasses and polishing them for a moment before she spoke. 'I struck a deal with Bulletar: if we could provide them peanuts they'd get us credits and trade ships.'

'And with whom did you "strike a deal" on Bulletar?'

La'Shay put her glasses back on but did not meet the captain's gaze. 'A man from the Corps. He provided us with a few Ultra-Reapers in exchange for a parcel of land to build a burbdome, but he assured us that if we could trade them enough peanuts, we wouldn't have to give him the land.'

'And how's that working out for you?' Farah said and rolled her eyes.

Dr. Winston said nothing.

They got back on the Ultra-Reaper. La'Shay sat in the front seat, Catalina and Farah settled into the back. The machine warmed up its grav generator and lifted them off the ground, then La'Shay piloted them back toward what counted for civilization on Wholhom in silence. La'Shay had told them there were a few other small settlements, but most of the population of Wholhom lived in Hearth, which was situated between the peanut fields to the east and briny sea to the west. A lazy river cut the town in half, and the colonists used the water to irrigate hobby farms. Catalina saw corn, beans, vegetables—even a few medium-sized trees beginning to bear fruit. The town didn't seem to have much in the way of commerce. Aside from the telescope shop Dr. Winston had mentioned, there was a doctor's office, a few machine shops, dentists, and a comm station for communicating with other settlements. The planet had the sleepy feel of a small town. People either tended their gardens, which filled every inch of Hearth, or milled around the town square. No one had shopping bags, or walked in the hurried gait of someone who had something to do. Indeed, it seemed the beehives that hummed here and there were far more bustling than the people who lived in the largest city of this planet.

Catalina wished she had something to say about the simple way of life they had, about the beauty of self-reliance, about how there hadn't been a need to rush because commerce would find Wholhom sooner or later, but the doctor had mentioned the death of Dr. Mercurian too many times, and it was eating away at the captain. Why was Dr. Winston so surprised about it? Patrick had been dead for months, more than enough time for the information to percolate through the inhabited sector, and even if it hadn't, La'Shay was clearly a hero-worshipper. She knew the entire crew of the *Artemis* by name. For her not to have found out about the death of Patrick was strange indeed. Try as she might, Catalina couldn't come up with an explanation that didn't sound paranoid. Was the institute trying to hide what had happened on Epsilon-V from the Corporations? Did the Corps get wind of it and smother the story so they could still build burbdomes? Was there another ship working on Epsilon-V already? Catalina had only questions, not answers. Instead of trying to solve these mysteries, she was stuck here until she could figure out Wholhom's peanut debacle.

While they drove, Catalina took out her tablet and perused a few news sites. She could find no articles of Patrick's death. Not a snippet, nor a mention, not even an obituary. There was also disturbingly little on Epsilon-V. Normally, each new survey was written up and published through the comms. Surveys were real crowd-pleasers. People loved to learn about whatever flowers and butterflies had taken up residence on a new planet, or if some other planet had an infestation of a parasite or bacteria that another planet didn't—and, therefore, made their own existence seem that much more palatable, but there was next to no information on Epsilon-V. Just a mention that the *Artemis* had begun a survey there and found unusual organisms, and more information would be forthcoming when available. No mention of the creatures, no mention of the strangely familiar atmospheric levels, and worst of all no mention of the late doctor. It didn't add up.

Catalina tried to shake the thoughts of conspiracy from her mind. She had to trust that the Institute was throwing their absolute best at Epsilon-V. Perhaps she was only distressed because she had thought *she* was their best. She shook her head and tried to focus. Glamorous or not, she had peanuts to farm and a planet to save.

# 15

The knocking on her door grew more urgent and Catalina got out of bed. She never slept well planet-side. She felt trapped, like an insect with its wings plucked off. She knew her fears were unfounded, but sometimes she couldn't help but worry that something would happen to the *Arrow* that she came down on, that she'd never get free of the planet's gravity well, and that they'd be stuck there with the scant hundreds of organisms on Wholhom instead of the thousands in their living library aboard the *Artemis*. She knew that Fin could send another of the seventeen *Arrows,* and that—even in the unlikely event that they all failed—the Institute had a whole fleet of ships that could get them back to space, or that Dr. Winston could shuttle them up to the *Artemis* on some derelict rocket. She also knew that if any of that happened, the Institute might decommission the *Artemis*. Catalina's year on the *Artemis* had been a good one, and she knew the ship had plenty to do with it. She couldn't wait to fire up the *Arrow*'s gravgens, launch it into space, and link back up with the rest of the vessel. Hopefully, whoever was knocking at her door was going to help her do exactly that.

Once awake, Catalina moved quickly. She dressed in her green Institute uniform, donning the brown gloves, boots, and belt and paying careful attention to her badges of honor on her left breast. Each represented a victory over the emptiness that had awaited humanity before the Institute had launched its

Seedpods to start the Interstellar Spring. Each was a reminder that humanity alone was capable of bringing order to that cold, dark chaos of the universe. Catalina shuddered to think what even humble Wholhom had been before humanity seeded it with bacteria, flora, and fauna. Nothing. It had been nothing. There had been nothing here but a small, briny ocean and a bunch of rock. Mankind had found no organism in the universe except for the life on Earth. There were no extraterrestrial bugs or plants, or even bacteria. Mankind had looked into the void of space, the infinity of the cosmos, and found nothing. Each badge upon her breast was triumph over that nothingness. Each badge upon her breast, a promise fulfilled to humanity. Catalina wouldn't even exist—she'd have been born into the nothingness if not for the technological prowess mankind had used to vanquish the void of space and the unforgiving size and cold of the universe. Catalina straightened her badges because she knew, with the exception of mankind and the life it carried with it, the rest of the universe only wished to unravel what sense of order there was to the worlds. That was why Catalina worked so hard to make life thrive on the 51 Seeded Worlds. The alternative was nothing.

Someone knocked on the door again. Catalina carefully slicked back her dark, curly hair and tamed it in a tight bun. She opened the door. Farah Relkor stood there, wearing the same dirty, green uniform she'd worn into the field hours earlier. Her hair was a mess, her badges nowhere to be seen, and yet, the grass stains—or in this case, peanut plant stains—on her uniform and the grime on her gloves also bespoke of mankind's triumph over the cold lifelessness of the universe. At least, Catalina hoped that Farah was here to tell her something along those lines.

'Captain, I've made a breakthrough.'

'Go ahead,' Catalina said, stifling a yawn. Despite her immaculate appearance, she was not an easy riser.

'The fungus! I've never seen anything like it before. Well, I've heard of things like it from the ancient tropical rainforests of Earth-1, but the Institute didn't launch anything like *that* on the Seedpods. Didn't see the value, but it evolved nonetheless. It's like I've always said, fungus is more an animal than a plant, but this stuff, this stuff is a predator!'

'Slow down, Farah. You're skipping steps, I think.'

Farah rolled her eyes. 'It'll be easier to just show you.'

Catalina nodded.

'In my lab. Come on.'

*Right,* Catalina thought, and fell into step behind the overexcited Botanist.

Farah's lab was a hodgepodge of various experiments. Plants of every shade of green, as well as a few shades of blue, yellow, and even purple, overflowed out of various growing mediums. There were hydroponic tubes running across the walls, beds of gravel, and cubes of transparent gel in which delicate plant roots grew. Huge walk-in terrariums boasted mixes of plants and mushrooms, the only parts of the fungus structure that could be seen. It was toward one of these fruiting structures that Farah directed Catalina. It was a slender thing, thinner than a pencil, with a shriveled top.

'Behold,' Farah said.

Catalina scratched her head, 'What am I looking at?'

'The fruiting body of this fungus appears normal enough, does it not?'

'Drop the showmanship and just report, First Officer. I'm not on Wholhom's day yet. I still feel like its three am.'

If Catalina's impatience affected Farah, she did not let it show. Instead she stuck a cup of coffee in her captain's hands. Catalina sipped at the hot drink gratefully.

'Now watch as I bring this peanut plant, grown in our library, close to the mushroom.'

Catalina watched as Farah did just that, and watched as nothing at all happened.

'Nothing at all happened.'

'Correct, Captain, thank you, but now watch as I bring this specimen found here on Wholhom near the mushroom.'

When the peanut plant came within 30 centimeters of the mushroom, it popped open and tiny wisp of what appeared to be smoke came from the underside of the mushroom cap. Spores, Catalina knew, but why, she had no idea.

'It can sense the peanut plant?'

'That was what I thought at first as well, but no. It didn't notice a specimen of the same species grown in our lab. What's going on is far more complex. Behold.'

On Farah's obviously prearranged signal, the lights dimmed and a hologram came up in the middle of the room. A green, fibrous stalk, presumably of the peanut plant, seemed to grow from the floor to the ceiling and slowly rotated.

'What's that?' Catalina's eyes locked on to what looked like a barb or spike that jutted from the plant. It almost reminded her of a butterfly's mouth, it was so delicate, but there was no butterfly on its hollow end, just an empty canal that presumably ended in a point inside of the peanut plant. 'Is that the spore? I've never seen one look quite like that.'

'Excellent question, Captain, I wondered the same thing. Now what follows is not direct footage, of course, rather a recreation of what I have observed already happening on the plant. Coupled with the fungi's ability to detect the presence I think it is reasonable to conclude that—'

'Just play the clip, Farah.'

'Yessir.'

A mushroom bloomed into digital existence a few meters away. A grid showed that it represented the same distance between the peanut and actual mushroom on the table. It came slightly closer, and when it did, the spores exploded into the room, filling the lab with globular balls floating around, looking for a place to land.

'They have very sensitive receptors,' Farah said.

Indeed, most of the spores, not seeming to find their intended target, bounced around and settled to the ground or were blown away, but one floated just right and bumped into the strange protrusion sticking from the peanut plant. As soon as it touched the protuberance, it latched on and began to expand slowly down the hollowed-out middle of the spike. It did this methodically until it seemed to strike a vein within the peanut plant. Then its growth exploded. Once it found its energy source, fine, white hairs filled the peanut plant. They slowly wormed their way through the inside of the plant, down the stems, through the roots, and into the nodes where the nitrogen was stored. Once there, the fungus stopped spreading. It reached some sort of equilibrium, taking enough nitrogen and sugar to survive, but not so much as to kill the peanuts. After a moment, it extended more of its thread-like mycelium through the ground and up popped another mushroom, and then the cycle repeated. The fungus was a parasite, living inside the peanut, gaining enough energy to reproduce.

'There's not a damn thing wrong with the peanuts,' Farah said. 'If anything, they're stronger than most if they've been able to survive this stuff for this long.'

'So, it's a fungus problem?'

'It's more complicated than that. The spike thing? That had me stumped. I looked through every database I knew before finally giving up and having the computer run a scan.'

'Unsuccessful?

'Far from it. Multiple results, took barely a second.'

'And?'

'It's the proboscis from an insect, left there somehow. My working theory is that the pesticides they sprayed were some new variety not sanctioned by the Institute.'

'You're saying the pesticides killed the insect and the fungus moved in? So if she stops spraying, won't the mushroom be unable to get into the peanut plants? They'll be locked out.'

'Maybe. I found this proboscis without anything attached to it. Its very resilient, made of a carbon network, actually—the computers think it's a diamond. I'm worried that whatever pesticide she used is making the beetles' mouths fall off. There could be thousands of the barbs already in the soil, and I have no idea how long they'll last. Really, sir, it's not a problem I can solve—its far more complex than I had anticipated.' Farah looked crestfallen.

Catalina nodded, immediately understanding. Yet this was what she knew she was going to have to do when they first lost Patrick Mercurian, this was why she had torn up Roman's letter and didn't believe his performance on the *Artemis* for a second. She opened her comm to Roman, but he didn't answer. Catalina sighed inwardly, then contacted Fin back up on the *Artemis*. 'Fin, get Ensign Jupiter to Farah's lab. We got a lot to go over. And prep Dr. Winston, looks like she has some explaining to do.'

'Err…Captain? I, uh, that won't be possible, sir.'

'Why not?'

'Jupiter and Dr. Winston left on an Ultra-Reaper almost as soon as you got back. He said he had some questions for her about true bugs or something. I'm sorry, Captain, I didn't know I was standing on orders to hold him here.'

'It's fine, pilot. You wouldn't have been able to stop him from up there anyway,' Catalina said, hoping her comm unit didn't pick up Farah's rage.

'That barbarian! Just think what he's going to do to that poor girl. He was already going on about her glasses. She doesn't stand a chance. By the juice of a peach, if Ken so much as glances at him when he gets back I swear I'm going to—'

'Enough, Officer. I'm sure we'll see Roman in the morning, one way or another. Until then, I want you to keep developing your theory. If a pesticide killed these bugs a few years ago, why are they still having problems now, and what pesticide would kill a bug and leave its mouth?'

'Captain, I think it might be best if we go after them,' Farah said through gritted teeth.

'We are not here to babysit our science officer. She asked to see an Entomologist, she's going to see an Entomologist.'

'Yeah, a lot of one.'

Catalina had never been so relieved to hear one of Ikamon's poorly timed jokes. She nodded at the Marine Biologist and excused herself from the lab, hoping he could redirect at least some of Farah's outrage.

# 16

Doctor La'Shay Winston found the Entomologist Roman Jupiter a tad unorthodox, but then she'd never met an Entomologist from an O-class ship before. When she'd asked him for a briefing about what the insects were doing to her peanuts, he'd only grinned wolfishly and raised an eyebrow toward her Ultra-Reaper. Hans Burbur, the resident Entomologist, beekeeper, mead brewer, and drunkard, had never looked at another human the way Jupiter looked at La'Shay. She offered him a ride out to where the beetles had last been seen ravaging the crops, but Jupiter had told her to keep driving.

'But this is where they're worst right now. I think it must have something to do with the nitrogen being fixed in the peanut nodes, but unfortunately I am not too familiar with, uh, insects.'

Jupiter had smiled so wide when she'd stuttered that she'd felt her face flush.

'I'm sure there is no one better suited to appraise and care for the poor *arachis hypogea* of Wholhom than your own marvelously magnified eyes. I would be honored to lend my humble expertise to your little operation here and thus leave this planet in a better state of balance than before I arrived, but first I fear I must get to know what grows upon this world. I have not seen creatures besides honeybees, humans, and these dreaded black beetles you've spoken of, and seen no plants besides endless rows of *arachis hypogea* and the fruit and vegetable cultivars you had back in your city,' Jupiter said.

'Well there's not much else. We tend honeybees so we don't need a native pollinator population,' La'Shay said.

Roman cleared his throat:

*'Ah, apis meliflera. Did you know that your humble work would make you, to your cousins, seem a jerk?'*

La'Shay cocked her head. Had that rhyme been intentional? If it had, it was an awful attempt at a limerick. 'It's not like we had any butterflies or anything. We're lucky Hans has been so successful with the honeybees.'

'I doubt that even the bright colors of an emperor swallowtail could compare to your beauty, yet I feel it is my responsibility to the Institute to see what has happened to the organisms that have made Wholhom fertile for peanut butter and honey.'

La'Shay felt herself bat her eyelashes. She had not been complimented by a man about anything besides jumpstarting an Ultra-Reaper in a long time. She wasn't particularly a fan of butterflies, but to hear Jupiter compare her to something he found so beautiful was refreshing and attractive.

'Mr. Jupiter, our crops,' she began, trying not to let her mind wander to how alone they were out here.

'Please, call me Roman, and the particular creature I'm looking for has little agricultural purpose at all. Tell me, do you have fireflies upon this world?'

La'Shay was taken aback. 'Fireflies? There might have been some in the reports, but I can't be certain.'

Roman's eyes gleamed.

'What significance can they possibly have to the peanuts?' La'Shay said.

'Probably little to none, but ecology has a way of doing things, and I'd like to see how it did them here before you so efficiently streamlined it.'

La'Shay rolled her eyes at that. Maybe Roman was burly and knew about bugs, but he also talked kind of flowery and didn't seem to know how to give a girl a straight compliment. They flew on, past the endless rows of peanuts, until they reached Wholhom's mountain range. These mountains that were but bumps compared to the titans of Earth-1 were what produced rain from the water evaporated in the briny sea kilometers to the west. The foothills of these small mountains still contained all the various species that had once lived in what was now firmly the domain of the peanut. The corporate representative who had traded La'Shay a promise of peanuts for Ultra-Reapers had said that it wasn't worth it to plow the slopes, so here they were.

'Here we are,' La'Shay said, lowering the gravs on the Ultra-Reaper until it came to a rest on the craggy dirt.

Roman hopped off and immediately began to flit from flower to flower like a butterfly.

'Amazing, simply amazing,' he'd mumble now and then, capturing something in a tube or shaking a few seeds into a plastic envelope. La'Shay didn't see what was so impressive about it all. Down below, a carpet of green was bringing commerce to this world, marred only here and there by the sickly yellow caused by the beetles. Up here, life was struggling to survive. Wispy grass clung to the reddish dirt, barely concealing it. Lanky flowers pressed up toward the sun and bland shrubs offered some texture to the otherwise drab scene. A few dandelions were the largest dose of vitality. None of the plants made berries, for there was no way to spread them. There were no nuts, because they did not travel well in the Seedpods with the technology the Institute had possessed when they launched them. That the plants had gotten this far up the mountain was impressive in a way, considering only wind had carried their seeds—as no birds had been introduced by the colonists—and yet, Roman was totally enraptured.

'Ha! You have spreading cosmos. An unusual adaptation, a treat! I wonder...do you have green flies? Those tend to do well. Pollinators, you know. Not showy like your butterflies, but useful nonetheless. And, ah yes...a few spiders, interesting you hadn't mentioned those.'

'I didn't realize they were significant to our problem,' La'Shay said.

> *'A spider's web, that's made of silk,*
> *proves many flies live and their ilk.'*

'What?'

Roman looked embarrassed when La'Shay didn't respond enthusiastically to his rhymes.

'I doubt spiders are significant to this particular problem, yet they are significant all the same. At the very least, their abundance proves you have a healthy population of insects here, or you did.'

La'Shay was getting frustrated. It seemed Roman insulted and complimented her with every other sentence. 'Have you got your samples? I have a planet to tend.'

'There's just one more thing I....there.' Roman grinned and La'Shay saw them.

Fireflies.

Just one illuminated the craggy foothills at first, but after a moment another replied back with an identical, yellow blip. A few others began to illuminate their abdomens in the fading light, and soon there were dozens of the insects glowing in the foothills. Roman carefully followed one with a sample jar in hand and caught it, then followed some invisible path until he spotted another insect, this one not lighting up at all, and scooped it up into the plazzglass jar as well. The two fireflies began to copulate, and once that was under way Roman turned to La'Shay, his smile wide, his eyes moist with tears.

'My dearest Shay, never have I stepped foot on a planet where these darling creatures don't exist, and here they are on your humble world. Miraculous, is it not?'

La'Shay shrugged. 'I guess. They were included in the Seedpods, weren't they? Makes sense that they're out here.'

'They were *not* on the Seedpods, or if they were they're not in the records, nor has anyone taken credit for releasing their beauty upon the Seeded Worlds. Yet I find a different variant on each and every world I visit, a trick of evolution under a dozen different suns, to be sure, but that is not truly the most intriguing aspect of the mystery.' Roman waited a moment for La'Shay to say something, but she did not rise to the bait. Roman was undeterred. He continued, 'This is the only plant or animal that is on *every world*. Not even the mighty cockroach can claim that feat, nor can any single variety of plant, well, except for algae and cyanobacteria, but those are everywhere—even Officer Relkor's not impressed with that. This creature, the humble firefly, is the only animal, save humans, to find a place on every world it has touched, and currently I believe it is outpacing even our colonial efforts. I do not know why or how, only that it is a miracle, and each world is more beautiful because of them.'

'So what purpose do they serve?'

'Little and less. They do not pollinate, nor do they serve as a protein source for people nor a particularly rich soil additive. They are, in my opinion, possibly the only purely aesthetic choices that went into making these alien ecosystem, and because of that choice I feel I owe someone in the Institute my life's efforts to go and find if they truly can survive on every world.'

'I doubt someone chose them because they were pretty.'

'But, dearest Shay, look at what they do to your glasses. Where before, all I could see were your beautiful brown eyes reflecting the setting sun so magnificently, now I can see the fireflies reflected back, making you practically sparkle, like stars lost in the darkness of your skin.'

'All you talk about is my glasses,' La'Shay said, removing them and polishing them on her coat, wondering when Roman had given her a pet name, and why she hadn't noticed.

'I had not fully appreciated you without them. Before, in the light of your sun, I found you beautiful, but now, under the stars, you are positively resplendent. Tell me, were you born here?'

'No. No one has been except a few dozen kids.'

'Then how lucky it was you found a planet that so perfectly matches your rich complexion,' Roman said, then knelt down and picked a few flowers. La'Shay recognized them as the spreading cosmos. Once in hand, he gently approached her and put them in her hair. 'There, see? What better color for your dark locks than the white and faintest touch of purple that the cosmos has? You are a creature of this world, as much its protector as any other, and I am sure you were meant to be here, as sure as I am that you were meant to steal my heart in these dusty foothills.'

'Stop talking?' La'Shay managed awkwardly.

Oh? Roman looked as if he wanted to say, but La'Shay was on him, her lips found his and they embraced, kissing passionately as the fireflies danced around them.

Roman started on her mouth, but soon as she let him he was kissing her neck, then caressing her shoulders as he slowly undressed her, whispering how beautiful her skin was underneath the light of the stars. He lay her lab coat on the ground perhaps a bit too smoothly, clearly an experienced hand, but then La'Shay forget everything as his tongue found her breasts, her nipples, her clitoris. She trembled with pleasure as Roman alternated between pleasing her with his mouth and reciting his heavy-handed naturalist poetry to her. Eventually, she told him to stop talking and he obliged, focusing more on kissing and caressing every inch of her naked body. Her skin tingled in the cold where the heat of his body wasn't pressed against her. Her skin tingled with anticipation.

'Are you sure?' Roman asked gently, and she nodded, and then he was inside of her and the fireflies blended with the stars and for a moment everything was perfect.

She came to minutes, or hours later, wrapped in her labcoat and covered in Roman's uniform. He slept naked on the dirt, a big grin on his face, bigger even than his erection. La'Shay considered him for a moment, how quickly he'd disarmed her, but she quickly concluded she did not really care. He was kind, intelligent enough, certainly handsome—in a roguish bear-like sort of way—and he had something about him, a refreshing blend of no-nonsense masculinity and tended femininity that made him seem perhaps too nonthreatening. She wondered how many women he'd been with before, and decided that while she didn't really mind, she also didn't really want to go again. She threw his coat at his penis and he woke up with a start, his wolfish grin growing sheepish.

'Nice moves, loverboy. Now we got a planet to save.'

# 17

La'Shay tried to argue with Roman, but eventually conceded. Dawn was spectacular on Wholhom, though the sunrise itself wasn't particularly beautiful. What little precipitation that occurred on Wholhom fell as snow on the tops of the mountains whose foothills they now stood upon. Cold mountain brooks were diverted to irrigate the peanut fields before joining together to form the river that ran through Hearth and into the briny sea, thus completing the planet's lackluster water cycle. Not many clouds floated through the air, so sunrise was lacking the garish purples and reds Roman assured La'Shay the other planets had. What Roman found so beautiful, and what La'Shay came to admit was beautiful as well, was watching nature wake up.

First, the crickets awakened. Finally warm after their long night, they began to sing. Then the dirt itself seemed to come to life as tiny gnats and beetles scurried about, racing for a meal. After them came the predators, a scant few spiders, vigilant after a night spent constructing their webs. A few wasps and flies zipped about, looking for less-alert individuals to prey upon. La'Shay had only the faintest memories of bird songs from Earth-2, and Wholhom wouldn't have the biomass to support them for years. She hadn't ever realized that, without them, the insects could still make so much noise. What was most impressive, though, what La'Shay—as a Botanist—was ashamed she'd never witnessed before, was the rising of the flowers.

The creeping cosmos especially were a treat to watch. Roman insisted that La'Shay look at the flowers instead of him dressing. He said to see a man clothed or naked was to see him at his best, but between states he was vulnerable. La'Shay could understand what he meant as he roughly tugged on his ugly, green-and-brown uniform, first hopping from leg to leg, then struggling to get the top half of the coverall zipped up and over his hairy torso. She understood why he preferred the cosmos. They did the opposite. While Roman dressed, the cosmos undressed. Each blossom started as a tiny ball that within a few moments unfurled into countless delicate white petals, touched with the faintest hint of purple, and a yellow center nearly invisible to La'Shay. She felt ashamed that she'd never watched this sensual display of brazen sexuality before, but then, she knew why.

Doctor La'Shay Winston was a licensed Terraformer, trained at the finest school on Earth-2. An entire planet, and nearly fifty thousand people, depended on her skills and knowledge of botany to survive. Her mission was to produce as many calories as possible to feed the masses, power their internal combustion engines to put a little good old carbon dioxide in the atmosphere to jump start global warming to melt the ice caps and energize the water cycle, and perhaps produce enough peanuts to start interplanetary commerce with Bulletar or Tanagra. La'Shay didn't have time to watch flowers unfurl, nor did she have time to chase fireflies or marvel at the color of a fly. She had a world to establish, beekeepers to keep happy, peanuts to grow, and an economy to start.

'Roman, it's time we talked about what's happening to my peanuts.'

'I agree. I'm glad we had last night together. You have a passion in you I find intoxicating, a sense of duty and responsibility that I'm sure this world will need to survive. I'm sure you'd stop at nothing to save this planet.'

'What is that supposed to mean?'

'I looked at your peanut plants while you were out there with the captain and Officer Relkor. I didn't know what to think, but now it's so clear. I forgive you, Shay! With an open heart, we can get through this.'

La'Shay felt her skin grow hot. 'I don't have to explain myself to you! The Institute was failing us. This has been going on for *years* and they haven't responded.'

'Just tell me what was in it and we can work together to fix what has been done.'

'I don't know what it was, just that it worked—that it had been working for years—and didn't contaminate the peanuts at all. Ms. Relkor couldn't even find anything wrong with them. The Institute is not supposed to be some regulatory body. It's too big and has too many missions. You can't expect them to keep up to date on every synthetic pesticide discovered out here. It's survival, that's it. We can't be bothered with biomass, we have lives on the line.'

'Don't think for a moment I don't care about you, Shay Winston, but my heart goes out for the organisms struggling to survive here as well. I believe they'll be able to protect you better than I can,' Roman said, and sighed. 'You tried to end part of the problem and you made it worse. Your big heart got in the way of your brilliant mind. The beetles were *protecting* your plants.'

'What are you talking about?'

Roman walked down the scrubby hill towards the peanut fields, then he turned and held out a hand for her to take, 'Come along, darling.'

La'Shay hated him in that moment, but she followed, her fists clenched.

'I don't give a shit about your damn beetles. I sprayed them with it and watched their little bodies melt into nothing. A DNA decombiner, that's what he called it. Said it'd break up the genome of the things, and it did. Too bad I forgot there's DNA in every cell.'

Roman plucked a beetle off of a peanut plant. 'These beetles mean the peanuts no more harm than I do you.' Roman tenderly brought the bug up to her face, as if it was a flower instead of a disgusting beetle. 'Look at its mouth, it has *mandibles*. This little guy is a predator. No doubt some iteration of the ladybug. And you know what ladybugs eat? Aphids, a type of true bug with a long, tube-like mouth that sucks juices from healthy plants.'

La'Shay's mind spun. 'Why would the Institute send aphids on the Seedpods?'

'They didn't. Not any more than they sent black ladybugs, which, just like you, are a beauty unique to Wholhom and don't exist on Earth-1 or any other planet. What they sent were true bugs, creatures with tubes for mouths, like cicadas. These evolved on your world, perfectly suited to it just like you— probably because you planted so many peanuts and took away whatever weeds they were eating to survive. Worry not, we *will* solve this.'

'But why would the Institute send an insect that eats plants at all?'

'In case you had weeds, or some virus came through, or maybe just because they're on every continent of Earth and provide a source of food, or at the very least, biomass. It wasn't intentional peanut-sabotage. I'm sure the tiny things evolved here, and besides, it looks like you did a spectacular job of eradicating them. It is curious, though, I'd have hoped to see a living specimen of the aphid. The Institute sent exclusively the larger variety of true bugs to use as a possible food source. Cicadas are especially delicious. Yet the aphids here are so tiny you never noticed them. Do you recall when they first appeared?'

'I didn't know they existed. I thought it was the beetles that were destroying the peanuts,' La'Shay said.

'No, they were just responding to a food source—helpless to their hunger, as was I when I first saw your beautiful, dark eyes. However, I fear our problems are much worse now.'

'What are you talking about?'

'If you've been spraying a genome decombiner on both the aphids and their predators, and letting that drip into the soil, where you say no trace of it has been found, I wonder where it went. Have you tested everything? What did First Officer Relkor say about the fungus?'

'That she'd never seen any so strong.'

'It's possible that through your kindness you unintentionally gave the fungus its strength. I don't know if we'll be able to fix this. We should tell the others. Unless...' he grinned wolfishly.

'Get in the Ultra-Reaper. Let's move.'

# 18

'And you have no idea who this person was?' Captain Mondragon's tone of voice was clinical.

'No, sir. Just that his products worked.'

'Goddamn genetech smugglers. You know what you did is an interstellar offense? You could have killed this whole planet,' Farah Relkor said.

'*Could* have?' La'Shay ventured a weak smile. 'So you can fix it?'

Colonists were always the same. Didn't think rules had a purpose until they broke them and needed help. 'First Officer, what's our plan?'

'Working on it, Captain. I've never seen anything like this. Some kind of chemical killed the aphids. Whatever it was melted them down to their genomes. I didn't even think that was possible, to split apart the cells of a creature and leave their DNA to be scooped up, but it looks like it is. Here's the weird part, though, the chemical left the proboscises. So what we have now is a fungus with an aphid's hunger for peanuts. How that even works is going to take me months to figure out, but we have more pressing concerns. The mouths of the aphids are made of incredibly durable chains of carbon. They're hard as hell to break down and they're everywhere. I put their numbers in the millions. It's like someone took knives from the bugs and gave them to the fungus, but only after teaching it how to expertly wield them.'

'True bugs,' Roman interjected.

Farah rolled her eyes and continued, 'The pesticide you showed us was this toxic chemical that for some reason was mixed with a virus that then took the aphids' genome and inserted it into the mycelium when they made contact, giving the fungus an appetite, so to speak. The fungus then spread this very successful mutation through itself, and essentially transformed itself from a transport network of minerals and nitrogen into a parasite.'

'Why would anyone do this? It sounds horrible,' La'Shay said lamely.

'Probably because whatever chemical they were dumping doesn't work on every planet. Insects adapt quickly, but the genes that hold them together, well that's another matter entirely, dearest Shay,' Roman said.

'Either that, or it was deliberate corporate sabotage disguised as a smuggler,' Kensei said.

All eyes turned to him. He shrugged.

'It was standard practice back on Earth-1. Introduce a problem, in this case the aphids that Ensign Jupiter cannot seem to explain, then offer a patented solution, this virus and chemical pesticide slurry. I say corporate because if it destroys the mycelium here, then all the better to build a burbdome. The Institute would have failed the Charter and the colonists' claims would be lost. I think the carbon mouthparts of the aphids are the smoking gun. There's no way anything like that could have gotten out here unless someone created it and brought it, probably whoever sold you the genetech to wipe it out.'

'I think that's a little farfetched, Ken, even for you,' Farah said.

'I don't know,' Roman said. 'They have the means and the motive.'

'How would the companies that build burbdomes and rocket ships know how to make a virus that can break apart cells?' La'Shay asked.

'Ah, your time on bountiful Wholhom has made you forget what life is like for those in the burbdomes. I, however, was just recently freed from one. They don't compost their waste and grow their own food like you do here. It's simply not possible with the densities of those things and how the labor is primarily geared to building more burbdomes. Some of their food is made hydroponically—leafy greens are tough to print—but the vast majority of the calories I had to eat to survive in that place come from printed white breads, potato paste, and nutritionally optimized meat from their protein caves. All of that is simple enough to create from human feces after it has been broken down into its constituent proteins by a bacteria with the proper digestive system. But worry not, we won't have to eat that slime.'

'What does that have to do with my aphids and fungus?' La'Shay said.

'The Corps are familiar with breaking apart organics, sweetheart,' Roman said.

Farah shot up, excited. 'An effective method of creating genetically modified organisms is to insert a desirable gene into a virus and then infect an organism—be it a plant, bacteria, or fungus—with that virus. The virus then inserts itself into the DNA of the host and begins to replicate, spreading the artificial genome throughout the organism as it grows. Really, what we're seeing here on Wholhom has happened on a dozen colonized worlds, in thousands of labs, millions of times. Every bacteria in the bowels of the burbdomes is a genetically modified organism designed to turn feces back into nutritious slop as efficiently as possible.'

'That's disgusting,' La'Shay said.

It was Farah's turn to shrug. 'I mean, we use GMOs in the fuel cells of the *Artemis* too. And the Corps, much as I hate them, probably just modified bacteria from the human intestine to achieve their results.'

'I still don't understand how this affects the fungus.'

'I'd imagine that whatever virus did this to Wholhom doesn't normally exist outside of a corporate laboratory. It's probably too unstable, and that's most likely why we can't find any trace of it except for the effects on the fungus. I bet if I had time and a control to compare it to I could untangle the virus from the fungus. You took a sample before starting all this?' Farah asked expectantly.

La'Shay shook her head no.

'All Botanists should take a control before attempting to re-engineer a *planet*,' Farah said and rolled her eyes. 'As it stands, I haven't found a non-aggressive specimen of the infected species, so there's no way to prove any of this in interstellar court, but Jupiter's right. The Corps are certainly capable of this kind of thing. They've engineered hundreds of bacteria, not to mention their meatcaves. The genetic transfer of the eating habits of an aphid to a fungus is less obviously useful than the transfer of the genome that makes a cow taste good to the artificial organism in their meatcaves, for example, but it's still possible.'

'And if Ikamon's hypothesis is correct, then it seems the Corps have found a way to profit off of destroying the ecosystems that have been evolving on the Seeded Worlds,' Roman said.

Ikamon nodded sagely. 'Before, the Institute was always called in if there were problems, but by putting your planet in debt first, then convincing you to do something illegal—and thereby sacrificing your claim to this place under the rules of the Charter—they would gain first a parcel of land, and then another, for the price of a few Ultra-Reapers.'

'And if they get a foot in on a planet like this, it'll be all theirs,' Farah said, shaking her head.

'Surely it's not that bad. We promised them land beyond the mountains. How will a burbdome over there bother us? I've heard Bulletar has whole jungles that the Corps don't touch,' La'Shay said.

'Bulletar is a hot, wet planet. By the time people settled there, trees had almost evolved from shrubs. There is plenty of water, and the plant growth is so fecund in places it regrows before a crew can finish surveying an area big enough for even a 100k burbdome. Wholhom, beautiful as it is, is a bit more fragile. A 500k dome would drain your water quick as anything. Which would mean no more peanuts, no more hobby farms. We'd probably have to buy their filtered water,' Roman said, then grimaced.

'It's fluoridated, you know. But try claiming you have rights to fresh muddy water under the Charter in an interstellar court. The Corps that run the burbdomes have interplanetary lawyers and five hundred thousand clients per dome. While you try to fight through the appeals process, the water cycle you're trying to establish is being sucked up for their showers,' Ikamon said.

La'Shay's eyes were growing wider. 'You really think that this is corporate sabotage?'

'This paranoia has gone on long enough. I will not be including any of this conversation in my captain's log. Is that understood, Ikamon?' Captain Mondragon said, hoping that her tone sounded as if she believed her own words. He shrugged, understanding that she wanted him to write down his theories, so she could see them when they weren't with a groundworm. Catalina was thankful for his easy-going attitude, but sometimes wished he had the tact not to speak so openly in front of people outside the Institute, especially colonists. They already tended to be suspicious of spacers, better to not make them doubt the ability of the Institute to uphold the Charter. Catalina had to redirect the conversation to what was at hand. There would be plenty of time for conspiracy theories on the ride out of Wholhom's gravity well and to Epsilon-V. 'You broke the Charter and messed with some highly unorthodox GMOs, but let's look at the big picture. What's the status of the planet?' Captain Mondragon said to her crew.

'Sir, the seas look to be in good shape. No fish, but a few varieties of clams, snails, and shrimp have taken hold in the briny water. The clams especially are quite delicious, sir.' Ikamon saluted.

'Sir, plant life is tenacious. There is a strong stock of wildflowers past the mountains, and the peanuts are doing great, despite being attacked by the predatory fungus. If this problem was diminished or in some way solved, I would deem this planet to not only have good air, but also healthy soil, sir.' Relkor saluted as well and stood at attention with her husband.

'Sir, there are some great looking fireflies out there, as well as a hungry and cannibalistic ladybug. I've never seen this exact species before, but I have successfully gotten it to eat a mushroom. I can't be certain if it's all black, or just one big black spot, but I have taken samples. The bee colonies they tend are doing very well. No mites. No colony collapse. Oh, I also saw some spiders.'

'Jupiter, your point?' Catalina said.

'Sir, yes, sir! I thought I had already mentioned it, sir, and was trying to show how healthy life here on Wholhom seems to be. I think La'Shay made a mistake, but now that it is fixed she will not make it again. I would like the record to show she is a passionate, beautiful woman with spectacular eyes.'

'Ensign, what is the damn solution?'

'Sir! The ladybugs, sir! They are cannibalistic, which means they are hungry. If we can show them the fungus is a better source of food than the aphid population that caused their population to boom, they can probably handle any outbreaks of the predatory mushroom. If they outstrip their usefulness, they'll just eat each other, the population will crash until the mushroom blooms again, and then the ladybugs will come to dine. I believe it will take a few crops, but so long as there is the native stock of insects for them to forage on between mushroom blooms, they should do a very good job of limiting the death of the peanuts.'

'God damn it, Jupiter,' Farah said. 'That's fucking brilliant.'

Roman Jupiter smiled so wide even Farah found it charming.

# 19

'So that means we can just release more ladybugs?' La'Shay said. Her smile was even larger than Roman's.

Catalina looked from the groundworm scientist to her own crew. Ikamon looked amused, Farah rolled her eyes, and Roman laughed.

'What's so funny?' La'Shay asked.

'We don't have any ladybugs,' Catalina said.

'And even if we did, they probably wouldn't do well here. But that's not a problem, we have all the ladybugs you need here on Wholhom,' Roman said.

'So, what, we just go gather ladybugs?'

'The problem I think is twofold. One, most of the ladybugs, besides my friends here,' Roman held up a flask of the black ladybugs, 'don't know how to eat the mushrooms, but I think that's a problem solved easily enough. If I could teach these ones, I'm sure I could teach more. The larger problem is that ladybugs cannot nest on peanuts. The texture is all wrong, of course, not to mention the smell.' Roman waved his hand in front of his nose distastefully.

'What are you suggesting?' Catalina said.

'Simple. When we came in by shuttlecraft I took a photo-spectral reading of the landmass on the other side of the mountain. It has roughly the same chromatograph reading as the foothills where La'Shay and I rediscovered the beauty of life.'

La'Shay blushed. 'That is to say, Ensign Jupiter showed me the bounties of Wholhom's natural splendor.'

'More specifically I showed you things you could do with yours,' Jupiter said.

La'Shay blushed even more furiously.

'Anyways,' Farah snorted in derision, 'What are you thinking, standard D and S?'

Jupiter nodded. 'Pretty much. I noticed you brought down some red gramma seeds. Can you afford that?'

'Yes, and some buffalo grass as well,' Farah said and rubbed her gloved hands together.

'Are you serious?' Ikamon muttered in Japanese.

La'Shay looked confused. 'I don't understand, you want to plant grass? Why? We have grass. What's a D and S?'

'A dig and swap. O-class ship talk for saying we're about to do a whole lot of work. Doctor, I believe you mentioned that you have idle hands on this planet. Summon them. All of them. What numbers are we talking here?' Catalina asked.

'I would think, assuming we want to keep production at its current levels so as to honor the Botanist's debts to the Corps and avoid collection, they'd have to start with twenty-five percent? Thereabouts?' Farah said.

'Darwin,' Ikamon cursed.

'I still don't understand,' La'shay said. 'We have to dig?'

'Doctor, due to your actions you have severely depleted the abilities of this planet to regulate itself. The toxin you introduced has caused the fungus that is supplying your peanuts with the nutrients they need to evolve into an aggressive, predatory species. My crew believe that the only viable option to save something of this planet's current ability to support life and its economy is to transplant twenty-five percent of your peanuts—over the mountains?' Catalina eyed Roman, who nodded. 'Over the mountains and replace them with transplanted wildflowers of some variety—possibly the cosmos in your hair.' Roman nodded again.

'But we have over a hundred thousand hectares of peanuts! We don't have the machines to process that much land. Transplanting all that would take the entire population of the planet—can't we just kill the fungus?'

'Impossible,' Farah said. 'At least, not without destroying whatever non-aggressive species of fungi you still have. We might've been able to try a virus, but considering that you're already being ravaged by a trangenetic virus, I don't think that would be wise. If we were to spray some sort of all-purpose fungicide I have no idea what it would do regarding that virus. It might mutate the bacteria in the nodes of the peanuts, or kill them off completely. I can promise you it'd kill both populations of fungus—the new predatory variety and the one that is supplying your peanuts with the minerals they need. You could try to plant all of your peanuts in native flora from now on, that might insulate it, but that amounts to the same thing really, and might further spread out your footprint, increasing a need for transportation it sounds like you don't have. It would be impossible to kill the fungus that is growing within your peanuts without killing those peanuts.'

'Our best hope is to transplant enough cosmos among the peanuts to support the ladybugs, but to do that you'd need a variety of year-round pollinator sources,' Catalina said. 'I know you have bees, but if that's your only pollinator and something happens to *them*, well you're in trouble, and we've seen it before.

'What we'll need to do is transplant approximately twenty-thousand hectares worth of plants among your peanuts. We'll focus on the cosmos and whatever wild flowers you have, as well as a good amount of native grasses.'

'We have to transplant grass? That sounds terrible! Didn't Mr. Jupiter mention something about seeds?'

'We'll definitely give you what seeds we can. If they do well, that'll save you some time, but we've found its best to rely on the plants that are already established on each world.'

'But this will ruin our economy! How are we supposed to harvest enough peanuts to sell to Bulletar?'

'You can still use your harvesters. The grass and wildflower mix doesn't have to be planted amongst the peanuts after this one time. That's why we recommend transplanting as much as possible. You can move the peanuts from this part of the planet to over the mountains where we'll dig up the native mix, creating a patchwork in both places, or you can simply write off the twenty-thousand hectares of peanuts and just bring in the native crop to save the majority.'

'We can't afford that. We're spread thin enough. The peanuts are all we have to pay our loans.'

'That's why we call it a D and S. You gotta move them both ways. Dig and swap.'

# 20

The work wasn't as bad as La'Shay thought it would be. Backbreaking, yes. Tiring, yes. Tedious, definitely. But there was something soothing about digging up thick mats of native plants, loading them on her Ultra-Reaper or one of the ground-bound trailers attached to it, and hauling the wildflowers and grasses closer to Hearth. After a week, the progress was remarkable. Instead of endless rows of peanuts, there was now a patchwork of rectangles. Peanuts dominated a few acres, then a smattering of grasses and wildflowers brightened up the previously vibrant, yet monotonous landscape. Best of all, the beetles didn't seem to mind in the least. They came along with the chunks of earth and plants that the population of Wholhom so carefully transplanted, and went about their work.

The aphids that had been afflicting the plants were nowhere to be seen, undoubtedly wiped out by the powerful genetech weapon La'Shay had attacked them with. Unfortunately, microscopic analysis of the soil showed that there was no going back. The soil was rife with their proboscises, which were made out of the ultra-durable carbon molecules. Ikamon stuck by his theory that the whole thing was a setup, that whoever sold La'Shay the genetech had known that the aphids had augmented mouths—were banking on it in fact—but no one else seemed to give this much credence. If they did, they didn't talk about it with La'Shay, at least not at first, but after a few days La'Shay found herself stooped over a pocket of cosmos with a hand shovel and Captain Mondragon moving steadily closer toward her. That she hadn't seen any of the crew yet hadn't surprised her. Thousands of people had taken to the fields on her command to save Wholhom's livelihood, though, in truth, perhaps even that was an overstatement. With everyone pitching in, it was likely they'd still make their shipment of peanuts to Bulletar, fulfill their debt, and thus keep their rights to their planet under the Charter. La'Shay realized that Wholhom was not going to starve. The planet was self-sufficient enough. There were hobby farms and plenty of peanut butter and honey. It was just that without their exports, they'd import less. They could have been living a life of ease if not for the peanut deal. All of this raced through her mind and, as if the captain of the *Artemis* had some sort of extrasensory perception, she sidled up next to La'Shay and probed along this very line of reasoning.

'So who set up your trade agreement with Bulletar?' Captain Mondragon asked almost casually.

'Some suit from the Corps. Said he could give us good money if we could supply Bulletar and maybe Tanagra with peanuts—that they'd trade us for high fructose corn syrup.'

'Some deal.'

'Yeah, well, try making candy without it.'

The captain didn't respond for a moment, but then said, 'You know, you're doing well here. Even with your little slip-up with the genetech, I can see that Wholhom is in good hands. You do the Institute proud.'

La'Shay found that a second member of the crew of the *Artemis* had made her blush. 'I don't think I'd ever have a place out there working for the Institute,' she said.

Mondragon shrugged. 'No. Probably not. You're a groundworm through and through, but that's what the Institute needs, people like you who are willing to do whatever it takes to expand life. I just hope that next time you remember that there are sanctions on that crap for a reason. Who's to say what will happen to that fungus in the future? Hopefully the ladybugs will eat it happily enough, but it could have been much worse.'

'I know I shouldn't have used the genetech, but how else was I supposed to feed Bulletar?'

'Why do you need to feed Bulletar?'

'There's going to be over a million people in those burbdomes within the decade. They need calories! All they have are organo-printers, and those are disgusting. I don't even like that crap on interstellar flights. I don't know how you do it.'

'Ikamon is a fine chef so long as he doesn't have to actually cook the seafood he serves, Relkor knows how to prepare every vegetable in the inhabited sector, and Roman works wonders with insect protein. We eat well on the *Artemis*, probably almost as well as you do here on Wholhom,' Captain Mondragon said.

'Well that's the thing, right? All those people on Bulletar are eating junk...'

'So what? That's their choice. They're the ones who wanted to move into that thing. We owe them nothing,' said Mondragon.

'But the Charter says...'

'The Charter gives colonists a right to fresh air, clean water, and either tillable soil or fishable sea. It says nothing about peanut butter, or beer, or vegetables, or anything else. The Charter is about promising people the right to work, because the founders of the Institute knew that in doing so, they would have to create a world around them that would, in turn, make their own lives more sustainable and create a new sort of economic ecosystem for the future. Whatever they are doing in the burbdomes has nothing to do with that. Bulletar has no need for peanut butter, just as you have no need for high fructose corn syrup. If you need it so badly you can trade for it or grow it yourself, but the amount of peanuts you are growing here is preposterous.'

'So you're saying not to export anything?'

'No, not at all. If Wholhom grows good peanuts, by all means send them to another planet, but don't do it at the expense of the health of your biosphere or at so large a scale you have to sell the rights granted to your people by the Charter. You can't let the biological systems that work tirelessly for you collapse. If the last of those beetles had starved, I don't know if we would have been able to save your world. I still don't know if we can, but because of them we have a shot. That is what the Institute is about, establishing and strengthening what were once considered 'natural' systems to a point that they don't need human intervention, and we can let them take care of us like they once did on Earth-1. Wholhom had that—at least that's what my reports say—but if this fungus gets out of control or you lose those beetles, well then that's it. Just remember, the miracle cures only work for a season, then leave you worse than you started. You're doing well here. Try to support a little more than just the peanuts and you'll find that you reap far more as well.'

La'Shay nodded as Mondragon stood up and stretched, pushing her hands deep into her lower back. Even after working the dirt, her uniform was immaculate.

'Doctor, I think that about does it. Farah has unloaded all of the gramma and buffalo grass. That needs to be spread wherever you have thin spots. She's loaded up peanuts for us to take and use if we need them as well.'

'We've only moved a few hundred hectares, there's still *thousands* more,' La'Shay protested.

'And now that you understand the importance of the work, you'll be sure that your people do it, correct?'

'Well, of course, but—'

'Then there is no reason for my ship and crew to stay here any longer. We have given you back your tillable soil, and I have faith that you will not squander it away and let the Corps establish a foothold with a burbdome.'

'Of course not! Especially now that I understand Wholhom's ecology is more than peanuts and bees.'

'Then our work here is done. We've fulfilled our end of the Charter, and you're going to fulfill yours. We'll launch this evening.'

'Oh,' La'Shay said, suddenly crestfallen. 'I guess I won't get to say goodbye to the crew, then, or thank Officer Relkor or Roman.'

Catalina rolled her eyes. 'This work isn't going anywhere. Go say your goodbyes, just don't let us be late.'

La'Shay nodded, 'Yes, sir.'

# 21

She found him among the cosmos, fondling one of the mushroom caps that had caused her so much trouble. He was covered in the black ladybugs. Gently, he coaxed one of the beetles down his finger and to the mushroom, where it tentatively nibbled, then began to devour the food source. Roman cooed at the insect.

'Roman,' La'Shay started, but the Entomologist hushed her. He held still until the beetle stopped eating, then opened up its hard outer wings—*elytra* Roman had called them—unfolded its delicate inner wings, and flew off into the field of peanuts.

'She's off to teach her friends,' Roman whispered.

'I didn't know beetles could share information like that,' La'Shay said.

Roman shrugged. 'Who the hell knows? Bees can trade information, as can ants. I'd wager beetles can too. We better hope they do, for the sake of our planet.'

'That's why I'm here, Roman. I wanted to say thank you, and apologize.' La'Shay took off her glasses and polished them.

Roman stood and looked at her with his complete attention. It was like being bathed in both lust and affection. His eyes dove into hers, searching her soul. His body seemed relaxed, yet ready for action. Certainly the bulge in his uniform was. 'There is no need to apologize for anything, except perhaps for removing those refractory devices which you know I find so intoxicating.'

'No, Roman, there is. I looked up to people like you, Interstellar Ecologists from the Institute. You were sort of my heroes, and then you got here and I lied about what had been happening.'

'You didn't lie, you just didn't tell the whole truth,' Roman said.

'OK...' La'Shay was growing frustrated. 'Look, I just wanted to say I'm sorry before you go. This world owes the *Artemis* its very existence. You all gave us a sorely needed reality check, and I personally wanted to say thanks for showing me the cosmos.'

'Does a daffodil thank the bumblebee for drinking its nectar as it rubs itself in pollen? Does the fungus thank the ant that so carefully tends to its needs before devouring its fruiting body? We are a pair as perfect as anything nature has produced. Thanks need never be said between us. It's as preposterous as a dandelion thanking the wind.'

La'Shay stepped up to Roman, moved within breathing distance of him, and kissed him to get him to stop babbling. She inhaled deeply as she closed her eyes and felt Roman's lips firm, then soften to stimulate her own. He smelled of dirt, mostly, but also of sweat, and of something undefinable, something darkly pungent that reminded La'Shay of the foothills which she found exhilarating. She breathed him in for the last time and let his big, hairy arms hold her close, pushing her small breasts against his burly chest. She'd miss him, his courageous bulge, his untamed hair. She'd even miss the fruity way he talked. He was unlike anything she'd seen on this world that she'd chosen to help establish, probably unlike anything a farming planet like Wholhom would ever see again. She'd miss him, she was certain of that.

'I just wanted to say goodbye,' La'Shay said.

'Goodbye? Do you have business outside Hearth? If you're gone long I'd like to spend some time with your beekeeper. I have questions about swarming on the outer planets, and perhaps could start a hive of my own under his guidance.'

La'Shay paused. 'The *Artemis* is flying out tonight. Surely Captain Mondragon told you.'

'Yes, she told me, but I told her that my place was here with you.'

La'Shay was speechless. Finally she managed, 'Wait, what?'

'There's still so much we have to see together! I have chrysalises in the *Arrow-5* to unload. Perhaps we can release them beyond the mountains and see if we can establish a wild butterfly population! And to think, I haven't even tried Wholhom's peanut butter. It must be legendary. And if you liked cosmos, I believe I saw *zexmania* ready to bloom. Tell me, do you have a wet season?' Roman grinned.

'But you belong on the *Artemis*. Captain Mondragon told me to make sure you get on it.'

'Oh, don't worry about the captain. She gets jealous when she sees me fall in love.'

'Wait. *WHAT?*'

Roman tried to hide his grin. 'I thought it was obvious. Maybe I'm rushing into things, but whatever! If everything took that attitude the fireflies would never light up because they'd always be waiting for another to start the show. La'Shay Winston, I love you. I love the way the stars of this world and the fireflies light up your eyes. I love the feel of your delicious skin against my own. I love your passion for this planet and how willing you are to listen to people who want to help. I love your vision, and your drive. I love your glasses, I love everything about you.'

'Don't you think you're going a little fast?' La'Shay managed to say.

Roman grinned. 'I understand if you don't feel like I do quite yet, because I don't see how anyone could love someone as much as I love you. I'm so excited about building this planet together. Just think of it, Interstellar Entomologist and master Botanist cum Terraformer, united in love, and one day marriage or civil union—or whatever you want, but preferably none of the old mono-religions, unless that's your thing, then I can learn to love that, too.'

'You want to get married?'

'Yes! Yes I do, I do!' Roman's eyes were moist now, his big grin shaking at its edges. La'Shay was beginning to grow concerned.

'Together we'll turn this planet into something amazing. With our love as the wind, there is no limit to where the creatures of this world can soar...and who knows, maybe one day our children will be able to appreciate the butterflies we release today!'

For a long moment, La'Shay said nothing. She let Roman hold her to him, his strong arms enveloping her until it began to feel like she was being smothered. It didn't take long. She felt the top of her head grow moist and realized Roman was gently weeping. 'I'm so happy,' she thought she heard him whisper, but dared not ask him to repeat himself. Her mind raced. They'd had sex one time—well, one night. It had been amazing, without a doubt, but now he wanted to marry her and have kids? La'Shay had never wanted kids. If she had she wouldn't have moved to some nearly uninhabited outer world. And Roman was willing to give up his life among the stars, just like that? She was flattered that he liked her, but also knew from Relkor that he had been with other women. Did he pull this crap on all of them? Somehow, despite all this, La'Shay finally found the words she was looking for.

'Did you say the chrysalises were on your ship?'

## 22

'I wish I could show you the library, but the captain has orders and has to get out of system. She says she doesn't have time to shuttle us back and forth and recharge the bacterial fuel cells. The *Artemis* is the most amazing thing. Big as a sports arena and filled with every insect you can imagine. Fireflies, ants, beetles, true bugs, flies, wasps, spiders too! Pity really, I'll miss it.' Roman shook his head. 'But compared to you and this world of yours it is but a petal of a flower.'

La'Shay nodded. She was getting tired of smiling. She'd called Captain Mondragon earlier, who'd told her to arrive as close to 6pm, Wholhom time, as possible. The captain hadn't seemed in the least bit surprised at Roman's newfound feelings. 'Don't be late or we're leaving without him. If you're too early, though, he might figure it out. We've been through this before.'

La'Shay hadn't been sure if the captain was entirely serious, but she would not risk being late. They arrived at 5:58. Roman was quite distressed. His babbling had grown faster and less cohesive. He was very concerned about getting the butterflies.

'Come on. We have to hurry.'

'Won't I contaminate the ship or something?' La'Shay said lamely.

'The *Artemis*? What are you, crazy? We got more bacteria on there than the Seedpods did. We're inoculated against just about anything that ever lived on Earth-1, and most of the stuff that's evolved since. I imagine you will be, too, after all the smooching we're going to do,' Roman grinned.

Shay wanted to vomit at his cutesy nonsense. 'Just get the butterflies. I'll talk to the captain.'

'Of course, Shay. Butterfly kisses?' Roman batted his eyelashes and La'Shay made herself do the same.

'Don't go anywhere, OK?'

'Oh, I won't.'

Roman vanished into the ship. La'Shay banged against the hull three times as she'd been instructed, and the *Arrow* of the *Artemis* lifted right up. La'Shay hadn't heard its grav generators humming, but was thankful that the Institute had machines that purred more quietly than her Ultra-Reaper. The ship got maybe ten feet up before a blood-curdling scream echoed from the now closing cargo door.

'Shaaaaay!' screamed Roman, his voice in agony. 'Damnit, Ikamon let me go!'

Even as the ship rose into the sky La'Shay heard clamoring and banging. Her heart dropped as Roman's head and one of his arms popped out of the still barely-open cargo door and he screamed his nickname for her again, 'Shay!' As strange as he'd become, she still didn't want to see him decapitated, though she did hate that he called her Shay. But the height and the closing door were too much for even love-struck Roman. His head disappeared back into the cargo doors. There was some more scuffling and yelling in another language—La'Shay did not know Japanese curse words, but from the tone it wasn't hard to guess what they were—and then Roman's hand shot out the cargo door one last time and dropped a parcel before being yanked back inside.

Despite the temper tantrum, La'Shay couldn't help but catch it. It was light and fluffy, hemp or some sort of plant fiber, wrapped carefully and labeled *Battus philenor* on a piece of paper in Roman's nearly illegible cursive.

'They're pipevine swallowtails,' crackled over her radio, 'beautiful like you—' and then the *Arrow* leaned back, blasted into space, and La'Shay was once again left alone. Except not exactly. She had the cosmos, and now, some peace and quiet.

After a moment of watching the *Arrow* fade into the sky, she looked down at the package in front of her. She carefully unwrapped it and found 22 little husks delicately wrapped in fabric. One of them was wiggling back and forth. La'Shay found herself overwhelmed with emotion as the creature slowly emerged from its chrysalis. It had dark blue, nearly black wings that sparkled iridescently in Wholhom's sun, and white spots along the edges of its wings that La'Shay couldn't help but think looked like fireflies. She smiled. Roman Jupiter. A man she never thought she'd be so glad to be rid of, and a man she knew she'd never forget.

# 23

The flight out of Wholhom's gravity well was far worse than the flight in. Farah tried to study the aphid fungus hybrid she'd discovered, but ended up just killing more peanuts. Ikamon spent his time cleaning aquariums for the clams he'd procured from Wholhom's oceans but scrubbed one tank so vigorously he scratched the plazzglass. Catalina worked on her report for the Institute, trying to pay special attention to the details of the genetech and the carbon mouthparts of the aphids they had never actually seen, but instead found herself writing primarily about Dr. Winston. Only Fin seemed undistracted by the stress the newest member of the crew was piling on the ship, but she was unshakable when flying the *Artemis*, and besides that, was as far away from him as the layout of the *Artemis* would allow.

They were all suffering because of Roman.

'He won't stop crying,' Farah said, incredulous.

'He stops to eat, and when he sleeps,' Catalina said with a shrug.

'And it doesn't piss you off?'

Catalina smirked mischievously. 'I just hope he cried this hard for me.'

Farah rolled her eyes.

Roman entered the dining hall. Ikamon was behind the Entomologist, pushing him.

'But I don't want to eat! I'm not hungry for anything but peanut butter,' Roman's tone was petulant.

'You cannot eat just that, you know? Come, try this.' Ikamon shoved a beer in front of Roman. Roman sipped it between sniffles. 'It's,' *sniff*, 'pretty good,' *sniff*, 'what kind of hops?'

Ikamon shot a smile at Farah, who rolled her eyes further than Catalina thought possible. 'Cascade, we got some a few planets back. Earth-3, maybe?'

Roman's face dropped. 'Shay was from Earth-3!' he wailed, inconsolable, heartbroken, a wreck.

'Captain,' Fin's voice sounded over the comm. 'We're free of Wholhom's gravity, well, er...close enough, given our crew.'

'*Perfecto*, take us to Earth-1.' Catalina immediately cursed herself. She should have given those orders to Fin privately.

'Earth-1?' Farah was incredulous. 'Why in Darwin's name are we going to that dump?'

'Captain, I assure you that I have enough preservatives to delay another visit home,' Ikamon said.

'Institute's orders,' Catalina said.

'What sort of orders send an O-class to *any* of the Earths, let alone the run-down original?' Farah said, her anger darkening her caramel skin.

'Despite Ensign Jupiter's contributions on Wholhom, he has been court-martialed. We are to take him to Earth-1 for processing,' Catalina said.

'Oh, well why didn't you say so?' Farah smiled.

'Captain, *gomenasai*, I must object.' Ikamon said. 'We have a duty to the Charter. We cannot forget about Epsilon-V for some courier mission, you know? I did not survey the seas there in any detail. There could be monsters worse than those that took Dr. Mercurian. Squid larger than even my ancestors could imagine.' The Marine Biologist shuddered.

Catalina clenched her jaw. Typical. If Farah was happy, then Ikamon rebelled. Far worse, though, was Roman's reaction.

Like a child denied a lollipop, Roman's eyes welled up with tears and he began to bawl.

'Oh cruel injustice! What have I done to deserve this emotional dose of pesticide? This unfairness to my very metamorphosis? I was living a simple, but admittedly flawed, existence on Bulletar, from where I was plucked like a flower not yet gone to seed. I was kidnapped, I had thought, with the noblest of intentions. However, now I discover that I will not be fulfilling the Charter as I did for poor Shay, but instead will have my wings plucked and be put in some horrid embalming jar on Earth-1! They say the pollution is so thick there moths can't even navigate by the moon. Oh, mankind is far more twisted than anything natural evolution has devised on the 51 worlds.'

'Captain,' Fin's voice came over the comms.

'What, pilot?' Catalina snapped.

'We're receiving a code orange from Juxor. Some creature from their oceans is eating up their carbon deposits and destroying their machinery.'

There was a moment of silence on the ship, then everybody started talking at once.

'I have been to those oceans, this is a new threat, and must be studied—'

'If you pick Jupiter over orders we could lose the ship—'

'Might as well just throw me into space because it's obvious we're not going back for Shay.'

The only voice Catalina really heard was her pilot's. 'I can get us to Juxor in ten days, and it's on the way to Epsilon-V.'

Catalina, like any captain worth her badges, knew how far Juxor was from Epsilon-V, or any of the other nearby worlds.

She had thought it would take a few days longer to get there though.

'A code orange is technically more urgent than Aprocrita's order to return Ensign Jupiter. It's certainly more important. Juxor's carbon is being used to build the inner worlds. Losing it would cripple our growth. Fin, fire up the Bubbledrive. Take us to Juxor.'

'Aye-aye, sir.'

'Now, the rest of you get out of here. You are dismissed to your quarters. I need you rested and ready by the time we drop from Bubble.'

'You don't have to tell us twice, Captain,' Farah said, slapping Ikamon's butt. He jumped, but smiled and walked a little faster. 'I love it when you fight back,' Catalina heard Farah say and tried not to think of the leather outfit she'd seen her in before.

Roman was turning to go. Catalina called out to him, 'Ensign Jupiter, a moment.'

Roman nodded weakly and stood there, shoulders slumped.

Once the crew had left, Catalina put a hand on his shoulder. He didn't so much as move when she did, when once that would have been enough for him to try to tear her badges off.

'You did well down there. Really good work. You understand why we need you up here, don't you?'

Roman nodded. 'Yes, sir, but if that's so, then why were you going to take me to Earth-1?'

'I can't just disobey orders. You did good work on Wholhom. If you do good work on Juxor maybe I can convince the Institute to let you serve out whatever punishment they give you here on the *Artemis*. And if not, you could always defect like you tried to do on Wholhom.'

Roman managed a weak smile. 'I somehow doubt I'll ever do something like that again. Shay was special.'

'And Betriz wasn't?'

'Who?' Roman genuinely seemed to have forgotten the woman he'd been in love with for the last year.

In that moment, Catalina considered their distance to the nearest airlock and what sort of weapon she would need to knock him unconscious.

'Oh...Betriz. You know, she didn't like the scent of fresh flowers? Still, better her than being with someone who is going to take me to Earth-1.'

Despite all her years representing the Institute, Catalina's jaw clenched strong enough to bend steel when Roman said that. After a moment of gritted teeth she said, 'I'm glad you could give up Dr. Winston for the Charter.'

'Really, I missed it, sir. I missed trying to help people and I missed finding everything life has turned into out there. I missed the hunt as well. Wholhom had fireflies too. I haven't been wrong about a planet yet. They really are on every planet. That video you showed, that truly was Epsilon-V?'

'The biggest you've ever seen.'

'Then there's that, Captain. Maybe we can go there before my court-martial instead of me defecting?'

'You think you'll be able to carry on well enough until then?'

'You kidnapped me from Shay, and my choice is either work for you, or you will turn me into Earth-1 at your earliest convenience.'

Catalina smiled inwardly. She finally had the slippery bastard. 'Looks like it. You know I heard they don't even grow angiosperms on Earth-1 anymore? No pollinators left. Nothing there but grasses and pine trees.'

Roman shuddered. 'I just wish you would have let me stay with Shay. We had a spark. Do you know what I mean?'

Even after Roman's blatant dismissal of what they'd once had, Catalina wanted to say yes. Yes, she knew what that was, and that she'd had it. *They* had had it *together*, but how could she admit it? She didn't dare say such a thing if Roman now thought of her like he did Betriz. They'd been together a year, and he'd lived as a groundworm for her. His six months with Catalina were probably forgotten long ago.

'If you need me, I'll be in my quarters,' Catalina said and turned to go. Part of her would always belong to Roman Luz Jupiter, but the captain in her was glad to see that what they once had had together was gone, and that Roman's old habits were back. Like a bumblebee in a field of flowers, Roman could never settle for just one.

The engine in the back of the ship hummed and then they were in Bubbledrive. Lights flickered through the port holes and Catalina smiled to herself as the universe ticked by faster than nature itself had ever intended. She loved her work and what it meant to mankind and was glad to have a full crew, even if one of them was a hopeless romantic. But despite his personal problems, Roman had proven himself. He was crew on the *Artemis* now, nothing more, nothing less. He had been court-martialed, Catalina thought with a grimace, but perhaps there would be a way to keep him on board until they could make it to Epsilon-V. What could be so important that Roman needed to go to Earth-1? Why hadn't the Institute sent them back to Epsilon-V? Catalina had never disobeyed an order from the Institute before, but then, she'd never doubted the Institute's devotion to the Charter that it was supposed to uphold. Catalina sighed. It'd be hard to convince the Generals back on Earths 1-5 that Roman was the best for the *Artemis*, but Darwin take her if Catalina wasn't sure he was.

She turned back once more to look at the silly-hearted fop. She had cared for him so much once, and thought he'd cared for her. Catalina stayed herself. This was what Farah had warned her about. This was what she knew she must do: watch someone she'd been naive enough to love chase other women without a thought to Catalina. She would have to do it for the Charter. She looked back at Roman, at his broad shoulders and stubble, his neat hair cut that was nevertheless untamed. There used to be a look in his eyes that seemed to say he'd give her *worlds* if she'd but let him. It had been so hard to watch it go, then reappear, directed at another woman. Catalina supposed she'd never see that look of wanton lust and desire directed at her again—except Roman's eyes were wide with it right now. *Why is he grinning?*

'Sola…I'm sorry, *Captain Sola*,' his words dripped charm. 'You said something about your quarters?'

'Is there something wrong, Ensign?'

'Tell me, does the Institute still expect crew to adorn badges?'

'Yes. If badges are to be awarded for our work on Wholhom, we'll print them ourselves and have a small ceremony on board,' Catalina said guardedly. 'Why?'

'Because I humbly request that if my actions on Wholhom earn me a badge, that it be your delicate hands by which it is laid upon my chest.'

Catalina turned on a dime and marched out.

'*Perfecto*,' she muttered as she left Roman and his stupid smile to himself and promised herself to never, *never* feel so much as an iota for the loose-hearted idiot again.

The End of Book 1

# Acknowledgements

First of all, thank you for reading! Readers mean so much to us lonely writers, and I can't thank you enough for reading. If you enjoyed the book, please share it with others and leave an honest review on Goodreads.

There is no way I could have gotten this story to where it is today without help. I would like to thank my beta readers. Brian Becker, I hope you find the changes to your liking. Hayz, thanks for the encouragement, girl! A huge thanks to my dad, Tom Mitchell, who edited this thing despite spending his days proofreading all day long. And then he edited it a *second time*. I cannot express how much that effort means to me. Thanks Papa. I don't know how you did it. Thanks to my mom for still believing that I can be anything I want to be. Thanks to my editor, Josiah Davis, who gave this book a penultimate polish.

Most of all, I would like to thank my darling wife and mother of my son. Raquel, you have the patience of an orb-weaver spider, the stamina of a soldier ant, and the devotion of a honeybee. I don't know what I did to deserve you, but I will work tirelessly to write enough strange naturalist poetry to make it so—or you know, let you and Leo eat my body if this doesn't work out.

# Diamondcrabs and Mangoes

Interstellar Spring Book 2

Available on amazon.com

www.jdarrismitchell.com

The metal pipe rattled and shook, and, like something out of the Wild West, thick, black sludge erupted from the ground. The group of organic engineers cheered. It was the third find they'd had this month, and if the analysis of the crude oil-like compound was anything similar to the last few underground seas they'd discovered, it represented billions of credits once refined and traded to the other Seeded Worlds. Juxor would continue to grow wealthy off of the natural carbon resources it possessed just beneath its surface, as would the men who came to this planet to help develop that resource.

'The priest will be happy,' one man dressed in coveralls stained black with the tarry sludge said as he twisted a gasket and slowed the gush of carbon slurry to a trickle.

'Oh, I already am, and outside of the worship ceremonies on the seventh day, I am not a priest, just a faithful servant of the Organic Church, and your planetary marine biologist.'

'Yes, Mr. Kane,' the worker said, smiling bashfully like a kid who was caught saying bad words and not reprimanded as harshly as he'd expected.

'How is it looking, Dr. Kirk?' Kane asked.

Roberth Kirk approached the hologram of Kane. His white lab coat had far less grime than the coveralls of the laborer. He consulted a tablet connected to a vial of the black, carbon-rich sludge. 'Very good, sir. Purity rivaling the old fossil fuel deposits of Earth-1. This is the best we've found on land.'

'It's as the Doctrine says, those who search will find what they are searching for,' Kane said.

'Mother Ocean provides,' a good number of the men in grungy coveralls muttered, an affirmation of their faith. Dr. Kirk frowned at the men.

'We need to get this cleaned up, Mr. Kane. If Dr. McKenna's hypothesis is correct we have very little time. A lightning storm is approaching.'

The holo of Mr. Kane laughed. When he did, the workers laughed with him. 'Osha's hypothesis, if you can call it that, has been proven correct only a handful of times, and has been flat out wrong dozens more. Besides, *Doctor*, you are hundreds of meters inland. You should be quite safe from any oceanic alien bugs, if I recall what Osha named them.'

The men laughed at that. Again, Dr. Kirk frowned.

'That will be all, Doctor. Now, leave the devoted to their work.'

'I have room for more,' Dr. Kirk said to the group of men.

Some of them looked at the hologram of Kane, but no one stepped forward.

'You have your beliefs. We have ours,' the man who'd spoken earlier said. Some of the men behind him nodded. Dr. Kirk sighed, climbed into a drone, and took flight.

From there, the perspective of the holo shifted to the camera mounted underneath the drone. It lifted up to see that the men, the carbon-sludge well, and the machinery were on a small island, and that to the horizon was nothing but ocean broken up here and there by other islands, most of which were bare and rocky, though a few supported tufts of green. The sky was a thunderhead thicker than anything ever seen on Earth-1. Bolts of energy cracked from the sky to the sea. The drone started to fly off towards the east when the Doctor started to curse.

'Back down! Down!' he yelled and hammered something on a keyboard.

Over the ridge of a sandy dune on the small island scuttled a wave of creatures.

'Enhance,' Captain Catalina Solaris Xao Mondragon said, and the holo obliged. It zoomed in on one of the creatures. It had a craggy exoskeleton, four legs, and two arms tipped with shimmering, dark, metallic-looking claws it waved menacingly. It was hard to tell its size, bigger than a man's hand certainly.

'The report says they're made of diamond—the claws are anyway.'

Captain Mondragon nodded. 'Proceed.'

The crab-like creatures poured over the sand dune and made for the machinery slick with the carbon slurry. The men didn't hesitate. One of them had a tool that sprayed a liquid on the crabs. There was a spark from the tip of the machine, and then the creatures were burning. They did not stop, but only added a high-pitched squeal to their unwavering march towards the men.

'Get on!' Doctor Kirk yelled, but the holo of Kane spoke louder to the men.

'If we lose this reserve their population could multiply. Stop them now.'

The men reached for their weapons. Some of them had projectiles that were illegal to transport through interstellar space. Others simply had sharpened pieces of metal. They attacked the crab creatures with mirthless determination as wave after wave scuttled past and onto the machinery that had found the organic sludge.

Their claws made short work of the metals and carbon composites that made up the machines. In moments, the pump was a pile of scrap and the black sludge was again pouring out of the ground. The crabs soaked their claws in it, then brought it to what must have been their mouths. Satiated, some began to excrete a black filament as others shuttled them around. All the while thousands more of the creatures poured out of the sea and over the dunes. The men's attempts to slow the tide of crabs made no impact in their numbers.

'Stop the flame thrower!' Kane yelled. The man wielding it turned off the gout of flame and for a moment the crabs coming at him paused. One of them waved a claw at its compatriots. A dozen other crabs waved back. Hundreds more mimicked these crabs. They all stopped going for the organic sludge and turned on the man. Then they eviscerated him. Their claws tore him into a thousand little pieces. Where one moment was a man the next was nothing but a pile of meat. The crabs gobbled it up greedily. Some of the crabs began to eat the sludge from the man's coveralls and excrete long, thin, black threads. One of them turned and waved to the thousands of other crabs. Thousands of crabs waved their claws back and did the odd little dance. Then the thousands of crabs attacked the workers.

We hope you enjoyed this sneak preview of *Interstellar Spring Book 2: Diamondcrabs and Mangoes*.

For more visit

www.jdarrismitchell.com

Made in the USA
Lexington, KY
08 September 2018